"Deny a m...
he'll want i...

Julio's sensual voice slid like silk into her weakening body. I want you, his eyes said. Without strings.

"Give it to him and he won't," Randall said apprehensively.

"I'm sure you know that rampant males will promise a woman anything to get her into bed."

"Oh, yes. It happened to me, didn't it? You were going to marry me. Once bitten, twice shy," she said coldly.

IN THE HEAT OF PASSION

SARA WOOD

MEDITERRANEAN PASSIONS

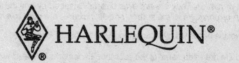

HARLEQUIN®

TORONTO • NEW YORK • LONDON
AMSTERDAM • PARIS • SYDNEY • HAMBURG
STOCKHOLM • ATHENS • TOKYO • MILAN • MADRID
PRAGUE • WARSAW • BUDAPEST • AUCKLAND

ISBN 0-373-80618-3

IN THE HEAT OF PASSION

First North American Publication 2002.

CHAPTER ONE

JULIO VALDEZ gave only a passing glance at the truck which had just driven up. 'Garden Maintenance', it said on the side. He pulled the brim of his straw hat almost down to his faintly crushed Marlon Brando nose and settled in the rattan chair to wait for something more significant. Like a blonde. It was his brother-in-law's adultery that had brought him across the Atlantic, not casual contract workers.

Air-brakes hissed, a cab door banged open and Julio yawned, bored with his tedious vigil. Then suddenly alert, he put his wine glass down, swung his Gucci loafers off the table and sat up, fascinated. The truck driver was female.

From the cab, a short Spanish boot had emerged, and above it a remarkable length of bare, womanly leg. The small foot waggled, searching gingerly for the rusting step.

Amused, he allowed himself the pleasurable diversion of admiring the shapely calf. A second satin-backed leg joined the first and his sensually curved mouth grew sultry as he imagined the exquisite feel of that tanned, flawless skin sliding under the palm of his exploring hand.

He considered the allocation of marks out of ten and his grin slashed the shadows. Twelve! Though he decided with typical cynicism that the rest of her would probably be a crashing disappointment.

She came out backwards, regrettably flipping down a swirling, navy cotton skirt to hide the admirable twelves from view. But there was the more than adequate compensation of a tiny waist that his hands could easily span. And a strong, firm body beneath the striped blue shirt that clung to her with pulse-stirring accuracy.

5

Julio's eyes narrowed, the smile vanishing. Those were strands of blonde hair escaping from the woman's peaked cotton cap and curling in appealing tendrils on the nape of her slender neck. He hissed in his breath. Could this be Santini's blonde?!

The woman turned. Julio had an impression of softly rounded, lush breasts before his brooding eyes reached her face. He froze in disbelief. '*Madre de Dios*!' he breathed in astonishment. 'Randall!'

Randall was Santini's woman? His sensual mouth tightened. The description fitted. His sister had been hysterical when she'd phoned, but sharp on the facts. About twenty-three. Five-six, well-endowed. Blonde, English, sexy. Randall...

Stunned, he watched her pull the cap from her hair and shake loose a river of golden waves, which tumbled in glorious profusion to her shoulders. Deftly she secured every strand on top of her head, the feminine lift of her arms and the bold thrust of her breasts making Julio's eyes drowsy with desire.

She was achingly beautiful. More alluring than ever. That unconscious grace had become an indolent confidence; the unrestrained teenager now had the face of a wanton, the blue eyes languid, the mouth full, pink, pouting. And he wanted her like hell. When she bent to check her appearance in the side-mirror and the extravagant mouth smiled alluringly with satisfaction, he felt the need for sexual revenge so acutely that he almost walked out to slam her against the truck and...

'*Maldito sea*!' he cursed. His Argentinian tan faded a couple of shades as he thought of his brother-in-law enjoying her earthy abandon, the luxurious curves of that magnificent body and its uninhibited responses, and slowly, painfully, he crushed the fragile wine glass in his huge fist in a violent explosion of uncontainable fury.

*   *   *

'I've cracked it! Broken the barriers at last... Good old Santini!' exulted Randall aloud, still intoxicated with happiness even though it was a full eighteen hours or so since her meeting with Carlos Santini. After an almost sleepless night, all the implications of Don Carlos's promises were just sinking in. Security. Protection. Above all, *prospects*.

Alone in the cab, she released some of her overwhelming joy and relief from the burden of financial worry by bursting into such loud singing that she almost drowned the deafening sound of the torrential rain which was beating rhythmic tattoos on her tipper truck.

Her visit to Don Carlos had put champagne into her bloodstream and bubbles in her brain. He was a great guy, warm, considerate... 'Whoopee!' she yelled, unable to contain her exuberance.

She'd become tired of making do and living in the cramped caravan in downtown Torremolinos, tired of touting for business and having the door slammed in her face. And terminally weary from being treated as a potential sex object by those seedy managers of the concrete complexes along the Costa del Sol, where she was contracted to maintain the gardens.

Santini's patronage automatically gave her some standing. Others would want her—and she could pick and choose which aristocrat, which wealthy wheeler-dealer, she went to next. Wonderful! A dazzling smile lit her face as she thought of her son's excitement, especially about the cottage Santini had offered in his grounds.

The rain was now falling like a white sheet, almost obliterating the steep cobbled road ahead. With great care, Randall coaxed the laden truck up the hill, worrying about the strain being placed on the back board that kept several tons of sodden topsoil from...

'Oh, *no*!' she groaned, feeling the weight suddenly shift. Slamming on the brakes, she leapt out to stare in dismay at the great heap of earth neatly dumped on the cobbles. Her tipper truck, way past its sell-by date, had

lived up to its name—it had *tipped*. Already the enthusiastic rain was trying to turn the soil into a mass of red
liquid. And beginning to succeed.

Ever the optimist, she looked around, hoping that a
team of navvies would magically appear. Nobody, but nobody was in sight. The only thing moving was the thun-
dering torrent which churned and tumbled through
Ronda's spectacular gorge.

'I've got to get *you*,' she said, scowling darkly at the
mountain of soil, 'up *there*.' Shielding her eyes from the
downpour, she glanced up at the fortress city of Ronda
which was perched—inconveniently for Randall—some
four hundred feet up on the great mass of rock above.

She sighed. 'No men around when you want them!' No
handsome prince on stand-by rescue service to flex a hunk
of chivalrous muscle, either—not even one of those
spade-happy Seven Dwarves to do a bit of digging!
Randall smiled good-naturedly. Not much could crush her
ecstatic, confident mood. 'You're on your own, sunshine,'
she said with a rueful grin. 'As always.'

Shovelling soil energetically, she got through four
songs before the sun came out and sent steam into the air
from her hot, perspiring body. It was then that she heard
the ring of hoofs on the rough stone cobbles. A navvy!
She straightened eagerly, ready to charm him from his
mule.

And dissolved into laughter. 'My prince!' she giggled.
Complete with glossy black stallion! Grinning hugely, she
watched the animal picking its way across the ancient
Moorish bridge below. 'Snow White, eat your heart out,'
she murmured in admiration.

He wore traditional Andalucían costume: theatrical,
flamboyant and calculated to make a woman's romantic
heart stir—skin-tight grey trousers, riding boots, a ruffled
white shirt and a short grey jacket.

The wickedly angled brim of his flat Spanish hat con-
cealed his face tantalisingly, but a Michelangelo jawline

emerged—cast in bronze, she noted dreamily. And from the consciously proud, ramrod way he held his body, Randall knew for certain that his face would be set in the required expression of dignified hauteur that Spanish men learnt at their fathers' knees. It made a nice picture. But...

'Useless,' she said disparagingly, coming down—literally—to earth. Princes didn't dig dirt. 'I'd swap you for the dwarves!' she added wistfully under her breath. And, she sighed, there wasn't time to drool over fantasy men, not with a hundred things to do before nightfall. So she bent to her task, perspiration beading her forehead, working like a steam train and panting as loudly.

There was a muffled thudding sound of hoofs on grass and then a growling, '*Puedo ayudarla?*'

A quick glance to her left from her bent-double position told her it was her prince. Laughter bubbled up in her throat again. Through the steaming curtain of her tousled wet hair she counted four black hairy legs with hoofs on and two black mirror-bright boots which were set apart as if the male legs above them were straddled. Very macho.

'*Puedo ayudarla?*' their owner repeated, a little tetchily.

'*No, gracias, señor,*' she grinned. Him, help? In those clothes?! 'I couldn't afford your laundry bill,' she added saucily under her breath for her own entertainment.

But suddenly the dark mass of a man's body was bending lithely beside hers, taking great scoops of soil on the spare shovel and hurling them easily into the back of the truck. Her prince, she realised, was Sylvester Stallone's blood-brother and Mother Theresa combined. Randall hastily modified her not unreasonably cynical opinion of grandees—Santini excepted. The half-Spanish Julio had been a monster. This one was a honey.

'Well, since you seem keen to help, thanks a lot. I'm terribly grateful,' she added warmly to the straddled legs.

'Hmm,' the man grunted in his throat, not breaking rhythm.

Taking surreptitious glances across at him as they worked in an easy harmony, she had an eye-boggling impression of long, lean thighs, the muscles flexing and contracting with startling elasticity beneath the clinging grey cloth. His boots were muddy now from the wet red soil, but he didn't seem to mind, working on with practised, economical movements. Briefly Randall wondered how a grandee had ever learnt to use a shovel so efficiently. Heaving peasants around? She chuckled.

'Enough.'

'Enough what?' Bent over still, she paused at the sexily growled word and shot him a puzzled glance. But she couldn't see his face because of his Zorro hat and her hands were too muddy to push back the mass of her hair that had fallen forwards to obscure her view.

'Stop.'

'But of course I can't!' she cried in mild amazement.

'Yes.' The word was snapped with the authority of a man used to instant obedience.

As if he knew she'd prove stubborn, the shovel was forcibly removed from her hands and thrown to the side of the track, crushing the cistus, thyme and wild rosemary growing there, each released fragrance billowing into the air and delighting Randall's appreciative nose. ·

Slowly straightening her spine from its labouring curve, she used her forearm to knock back her heavy fall of shimmering hair and found her startled eyes inches from a sensationally tanned male throat—which she paused to admire because it was as smooth as rich brown satin and quite perfectly contrasted with the blinding whiteness of his open-necked shirt.

Randall blinked. Handsome but arrogant... 'Let's get this straight,' she said patiently. 'I don't let other people do my work for me...'

Her voice faded. She suddenly had an uneasy premonition about the man's identity. The strong chin and shadowed face. The extravagantly curved mouth. Deeply grooved upper lip. Broken nose... She forgot to breathe. Till her body rebelled and finally forced her to take in a great gulp of air.

'Julio!' she cried in astonishment. '*Julio*?'

'Straight As for intelligence as always,' he drawled sarcastically and she flushed at the reference to her minimal education.

No prince. The monster himself. Her joy evaporated. She felt her face tighten as if the skin had shrunk, and her mouth had crimped as though she'd taken a bite of poisoned apple. Julio, she thought, struggling for comprehension. Of all people.

Randall's knees weakened, as the implications of his sudden appearance hit her with a force that rocked her world. If he ever knew about Tom...! Appalled, she found her protective instincts coming to her rescue. 'Whatever are you doing here?' she asked, sounding almost normal.

'Wishing I weren't.'

The cutting remark put the bone back in her legs. He didn't like Spain after living in Argentina all his life and wouldn't stay long. Her tense face relaxed in relief. Her secret was safe. 'Andalucía isn't to everyone's taste. Perhaps you should go home and pick pampas grass,' she suggested hopefully, her voice a little croakier than she would have liked.

'I breed bulls,' he corrected in world-weary tones.

'More machismo in that,' she commented sagely and forced her heart to slow down. Good news; he definitely hadn't upped sticks and moved to Spain or he would have corrected her on that, too. What a relief! She shaped her mouth into a beaming smile, her world almost spinning on its axis again. 'On holiday?' she hazarded.

His eyes flickered. 'Business,' he said with cold detachment.

'Oh. Long way to come.' Talk about blood out of a stone! It annoyed her how surly he was. It was as if there had been no childhood friendship, no love between them, no tempestuous affair—not even the final, shattering betrayal that had changed her life so dramatically. But then she'd lost her childhood sweetheart, the man she'd loved, the father of her child.

Whereas he'd merely seduced and then dumped the gardener's daughter. No big deal. Hardly surprising that he was behaving for all the world as though they'd met once at a cocktail party, exchanged pleasantries and had drifted on to nibble lobster canapés!

'Staying long?' she asked, trying to sound casual. But his answer mattered. More than he'd ever know and the waiting was making her hands tremble.

'As long as it takes,' he answered grimly.

Not so good, she thought, hoping her face didn't show its disappointment. 'How...how long would that be?' Acting unconcerned had turned her voice into a falsetto and she worried that he'd sense something was wrong.

He unfurled a cynical smile. 'Depends. There's someone I might need to flay alive before I go home.'

'Sounds messy.' Although startled by his malevolent tone, she managed to smile back. She badly needed to prise more information out of him.

'It will be,' he agreed, with an unholy relish. His eyes mocked hers. 'Unless she takes the hint and runs like hell.'

Every muscle in her body tensed. Did he mean her? Did he know about Tom after all? 'She? Bullying defenceless women, are you?' she asked shakily.

'She's as defenceless as you are,' he growled. 'Don't worry. I believe in justice. I'll only beat her raw if I find that she deserves it. Don't you think that people ought to be punished for their transgressions?'

'Oh, yes,' she said with heavy significance, hoping her eyes were telling him he ought to be roasted over hot coals if there were any justice in the world. 'Life normally does that, though. Fate tends to take a hand—'

'I can't wait that long,' he said curtly. 'I think revenge should be quick, hot and brutal. Shall we deal with you?'

Her palms went clammy and cold. He did know, she thought in panic! 'Revenge...?' She swallowed. For denying him his son? 'Quick, hot and...!' Covered in confusion, Randall let her words peter out, suddenly more afraid of the alarmingly menacing Julio than she could have believed possible.

'Brutal,' he supplied for her in a soft growl. 'How odd that you should connect yourself with my need for revenge. Guilty about something, are you?'

Admitting nothing, she stalled. 'Just trying to unravel your meaning,' she said with a ghastly smile.

'I ran what I thought were two totally unconnected statements together. I'm offering to finish removing the mess you've left on the road,' he explained glibly. 'Sit on the wall while I clear up.'

'Maybe once I was stupid enough to let you order me around. It doesn't mean you can do so now. I'm not sweet seventeen any longer and I decide on when I take a break,' she said resentfully, gearing up for the battle of independence.

'But you're sweating.'

It was a flat, dreadfully ungentlemanly statement and had the effect of making her mouth open and close in astonishment. Ruefully she remembered that, long ago, she'd mentally planned on what she'd be wearing when they met up again: a black, slinky sheath with a fish-tail and a strapless top that *slayed* him. She'd smile coolly, pass the time of day, watch his eyes fall off their stalks and sashay away in a seamless glide with some gorgeous hunk. But here she was, plastered in mud and sweat!

'Of course I'm sweating! I've shifted half of Spain into the back of this truck,' she grumbled, sweeping an arm across her damp brow and wiping her hands briskly on her grubby shorts. 'What do you expect?'

He looked her up and down disparagingly. 'A little restraint, for a start.'

'What am I supposed to restrain?'

Julio expelled a rasping breath from his lungs but nothing in his face told her why—until she realised he was staring at the V of perspiration on her shirt. V for valley, she thought ruefully, noting its accuracy in marking the shape of her cleavage. And although her plastered-on top and shorts had partially dried, they still seemed alarmingly attached to every inch of her body.

Was that why his breathing rate had upped to rapid? Just in case, she surreptitiously wriggled her hips to separate her hot flesh from the clinging cloth and plucked at her T-shirt to lift it from her body. Julio's brooding eyes honed in on her breasts with the accuracy of an Exocet missile and she shifted her feet because something was making her tingle in places she'd forgotten about.

'Very sexy, Randall,' he said with soft disdain. 'Learnt a few useful manoeuvres, I see.' Cynically he transferred his gaze to her wet-slicked legs, inching up them with agonising thoroughness and then slowly burning a path up her loins, her flat stomach and the unintentionally alluring V. 'Try repressing your sexual messages. This is inland Andalucía, not St Tropez. You're asking for trouble, going around like that,' he frowned.

But he'd enjoyed looking, she thought rebelliously. Sexual messages indeed! Didn't he realise how practical her clothes were? 'My frou-frou dress and lace mantilla are in the wash,' she told him crossly and he scowled at her sarcasm. 'Oh, come on, Julio! Lighten up!' she cried in exasperation. 'You're behaving like a Victorian male who bellows at his wife for exposing her ankles—and then pushes off to the brothel! I'm a working girl. It's hot, shifting soil. If you don't like what you see, don't look so hard. I swear you've been counting my vertebrae.'

'I didn't get as far as your backbone,' he drawled. 'And it's hard not to stare, with so much flesh on display. It rather draws the eyes. And even the little that's covered is competing for Miss Wet T-shirt of Europe,' he added with a lashing sarcasm.

'It rained,' she muttered defiantly, determined not to be crushed. Not this time. Even if, she thought irritably, he was looking at her as though she'd crawled out of the soil and was heading for the nearest slug pellet.

'So I see.'

There was such a chilling condemnation in his expression that she moved back and crossed her hands defensively over her apparently offending breasts, her blue eyes round and more than a little troubled. He'd become puritanical. Priggish, even. This, from the unconventional, free-spirited Julio! It was astounding, she marvelled, how marriage had changed him.

Or...was it that he thought the mother of his child should be in ankle-length skirts and a high-necked blouse? Randall bit her lip. She was getting paranoiac. He couldn't know about Tom, she reasoned. How could he? He'd have her by the throat and shake the daylights out of her if he suspected anything. She expelled a long breath, feeling her muscles release some of their tension.

Julio continued to survey her down the length of his nose as if he wanted to remind her of the distance between them, to impress on her that his parents had been aristocrats, his father Spanish, his mother Argentinian. Randall mused that he came from a family that had practised being haughty for centuries and in Julio they'd just about perfected their act! Out came a sudden irrepressible smile that seemed to annoy him.

'I hope I haven't said something funny,' he said coldly.

'Good grief, no! I don't think there's much danger of that,' she said wryly. 'I was only thinking that we must look rather an odd pair, standing here together. The lord and the peasant. You in your *Carmen* outfit, me in my rags.' There was the suspicion of a smile in his eyes and then a blankness and she thought she must have imagined it.

'In the absence of a change of rags, I suggest you protect the sensibilities of the decent citizens of Ronda by sitting in the sun and getting yourself decently dry,' he said with cold pomposity.

'Oh. I don't look *that* bad, do I?' she asked anxiously, going pink with embarrassment.

'You were never very good at knowing where to draw the line,' he frowned. 'Your background, I suppose. You had a remarkably unrestricted upbringing—'

'Don't you dare criticise my father, Julio!' she warned huffily. To her fury, her old inferiority complex was rearing its ugly head. Self-assured, blindingly well-educated socialites still had that effect on her, she thought gloomily, however hard she pretended otherwise. As always, her reaction was to fight back. 'Dad brought me up to be happy and to value freedom. He taught me a lot of wonderful, useful things that book-learning never could. I wouldn't swap his teaching for sophistication and petty rules about which wine to drink with chocolate pudding and how to address a bishop!' she finished truculently.

'I made an observation, nothing more,' he replied coldly. 'Your blithe ignorance of the way your body moves and how it makes demands on masculine self-control is disconcerting. I think you'd better sit on that wall and cool down, don't you?' he added in a low, throaty murmur.

Privately she had to admit that she needed the wall. Her legs seemed to have mislaid their bones for a moment. She hoped that was due to the heat—not the combination of his crushing presence and the appalling thought that he'd discovered her secret—or would do so any moment. Grimly Randall quelled the sharp pang of fear.

'If you want to earn your Boy Scout badge for good deeds, go ahead,' she said airily, hoping he wouldn't notice the tremor in her voice. 'Be my guest.'

Her mud-caked fingers reached out for the wall, closing over the rough stone with relief. And then she stood for a moment, taking a deep stilling-down breath, searching for strength to hold herself together till Julio rode out of her life again.

'Let me help you up.' Two massive hands appeared on either side of her small waist, their fingertips almost meeting.

Randall looked down at them in some alarm. Despite the formality of his tone, his hands seemed to be squeezing with over-friendly enthusiasm. A kick of memory sped through her body. She in the oak tree, he lifting her down, smiling into her eyes...

'Julio! Let go!' she snapped.

Questing firm fingers splayed out to test the rise and fall of her ribs. 'You're panting,' he murmured.

She blinked. She was. His fingers were visibly heaving. 'I sweat, I pant—you're very absorbed in noticing what I do, aren't you?' she grumbled, over her shoulder.

'Fascinated by every movement you make,' he said softly, and she tensed.

Ignoring her protests, his hands increased their pressure and her rigid body was being turned in mid-air and lifted as though she weighed nothing. Across her spine she felt the iron strength of a muscular forearm. A tremor of shameless feminine delight shimmied through her. With her hands fluttering on his shoulders, she looked down on his familiar, once-loved face and felt herself trembling. Exhaustion it wasn't. But she wished it were.

Because Julio was weaving his magic again, casting the same spell on her that had enslaved her so disastrously once before. She was getting too many stimulating sensations. They were combining with the wild sense of joy that Santini had released in her and were beginning to break down the dogged resistance she'd put up towards any dangerously attractive male who'd wandered across her path since Julio had abandoned her.

But no other man had been able to disrupt her senses as easily as Julio. A touch, a glance, a murmur of his husky voice dipped in honeyed brandy and resistance melted inside her.

Ashamed that her hormones refused to recognise that he was married, Randall felt torn between the urge to escape him and the need to stick this out a little while longer. Her heart thudded with the menacing sense of danger. But she had to discover his future plans or Tom might be at risk.

'I'm only out of breath because…' She searched for an excuse. 'Well, you know how it is, when you dance all night, come home with the bread and then do a full day's work,' she burbled, ridiculously anxious to suggest that she was much sought-after and partying non-stop. Why? she asked herself, puzzled that she should want to make him jealous.

Self-defence. Pride, she decided. It was important to her that Julio shouldn't think for a minute that he meant anything to her. Stupidly she wanted him to believe that she spent her leisure time fighting off husky young millionaires. If only!

His eyes had narrowed. The rest of his face seemed cast in stone. 'That explains it.' He paused. 'Gets you in the knees, doesn't it?' he said in a lazily suggestive tone.

She hoped he meant the dancing but suspected from his mocking mouth that he was referring to sex. Desperately she sought for some sex-dispelling humour. 'Actually, no. My feet. Plays havoc with my corns,' she said as solemnly as she could.

'You never had corns in your life.' Slowly he brought her down and for a delirious second he balanced her briefly against the soft cloth of his jacket. 'I remember clearly that your feet are perfectly formed from being barefoot as a child.'

The whole of her thinly clad side was welded by heat to the outthrust of his chest and then she was being settled firmly on the wall. Where she clung as if it might save her from drowning because she was frantically trying to kill the memory of Julio erotically licking each toe...

'Uhhh!'

'Do you feel all right?' Julio murmured solicitously, his hand gently testing the temperature of her forehead.

'Terrific,' she said firmly, grabbing his wrist and drawing the intrusive hand away.

'I thought you...shuddered,' he husked.

'Sort of. The hot stone burnt my thighs,' she said shortly.

His dark lashes lifted slowly. 'In the old days, you would have clambered up without hesitation.' She stared, remembering. Clambering up every tree within five miles... Kissing in leafy, concealing branches with the whole of Broadfield School set out below them and half the masters searching for Julio... 'You have a lot of stamina, I know. It must have been one hell of a night,' growled Julio.

Their eyes met full blast. Hers were startled and bright blue to match the sky. His... She frowned and shrank back. They were as cold and as remote as the snow-capped Sierra Nevada.

Abruptly he turned and she found herself staring at his back. It looked tense. Angry even. He began to shovel grimly at the pile of dark red soil, still heavy from the rain, and she wondered why he bothered and how she could idly broach the subject of where he was staying.

She felt crushed that he hadn't asked even one question about her: how she was, what she was doing there. She wanted to know so much—had he, for instance, told the Condesa Elvira that he'd jilted his childhood sweetheart? 'Is—er—your wife here with you?' she asked, affecting a matey, chatty manner.

'No,' he grunted on an outbreath. He shot her a filthy look. 'Why?'

Nothing matey about that. 'Just trying to be civil-
ised—' she began to explain.

'I'm not discussing Elvira with you,' he said coldly.
'So save your vocal cords.'

'Oh.' She chewed her lower lip, debating the wisdom
of the question she burned to ask. Wisdom lost. 'OK. I
can understand you want to keep your private life to yourself,' she said, managing to hold an even tone. 'But I think
at the very least you owe me an explanation. Surely I have
a right to know why you left me so—so—' She clenched
her jaw to divert her mind from the welling emotions.
'You dumped me without an explanation and the next I
knew was that you'd got married. Yet the last time we
were together...' Unable to finish, choked with distress,
she pretended to be overcome by a fit of coughing.

Her heart was flinging itself against her ribs, making
her short of breath. Every small detail of their last evening
had cruelly filled her mind and the memory of her anguish
was making her head spin. The scene was crystal-sharp.
He'd made love to her in a meadow filled with wild flowers and their parting had been tender, lingering, full of
promises. *Swine*!

Julio straightened slowly, his shoulders high. From the
way his knuckles whitened on the handle of the shovel,
it seemed as if he wanted to fling it at her. 'Whatever
your right to know, I don't think you'd like to hear,' he
said curtly.

'Yes, I would. I've wondered for five and a half years,'
she replied in a low voice. 'I feel I can't properly close
the door on our disastrous relationship till I know. It was
so unexpected, so sudden... When did you meet Elvira?'

'In Argentina. When she was born.'

'Oh. You never mentioned her.' With difficulty, she
controlled her trembling lips.

'There wasn't time to list all my distant relatives,' he
drawled sarcastically.

'Did you marry for duty or—or love?' she asked in a cracked voice.

'Both,' he said crushingly and returned to his task.

Ashen-faced, mercifully unobserved, Randall let her body sag. She'd asked for the truth and got it straight on the chin. She had no one else to blame if she felt miserable as a result. Elvira had probably been marked out for Julio from birth.

So Julio had enjoyed his fling with the gardener's daughter, issuing promises he could never fulfil. What did that matter? To him, a haughty grandee, she was nothing, nobody. He could marry Elvira with a clear conscience.

Angrily she watched the supple flow of his body as he worked, his movements more lithe and sensual than she remembered. A small curl of heat began to fan out from her loins and she killed it stone-dead, infuriated by her disturbingly carnal reaction.

There was a compellingly male air of assurance and authority about him, presumably acquired from owning those thousands of acres of Argentina which his wife had inherited and he'd added to his own. He lived in a different world. It wasn't surprising that he was treating her like dirt. He'd always had more adoration than was good for him, she thought resentfully. As a boy he'd been the centre of attention. A star pupil, adored by all. Boys, masters, matrons... The strings of Randall's memories jerked taut.

A wistfully gentle smile lit her face with the memory of watching him in rugby matches from the cover of the shrubbery, hugging herself with delight when his limpid dark eyes had sought hers for approval...

'It's done.'

He came to stand in front of her, interrupting her dreams of the carefree days at the boarding-school. Randall forced her mind back to the present. No approval was forthcoming now. Tipping up her chin, she made an enormous pride-saving effort to be cheerful. Her ordeal was nearly over apart from a couple more probing questions to set her mind at rest as far as Tom was concerned.

'Thanks. I'm terribly grateful,' she said politely.

Julio sounded stiff and formal when he spoke. 'You're welcome. It was the least I could do.'

'True,' she said ruefully.

'Don't push it, Randall,' he said softly. 'I've just done you a favour.'

'And beautifully,' she enthused insincerely. 'You've missed your vocation, you know. You'd make a good navvy.' She prattled on to show how little he affected her now. 'If your family ever gets the cold shoulder from your society friends because of some terrible scandal—'

'*What* did you say?'

'Joke!' she said, astonished that he'd taken her literally. 'I was kidding that you could get a job—'

His furious glare cut her off. 'If you're planning something underhand—'

'Sure I am,' she teased, determined to make him smile. She adopted a ridiculously melodramatic tone. 'The downfall of the House of Quadra— *Owwww*!' Julio's hands were gripping her arms so tightly that she thought her bones would be pulped. The pain brought tears to her eyes which she angrily willed away. 'Brute!' she gasped furiously.

His eyes glittered up at her, as dark as Broadfield lake at midnight. 'I don't know if you're joking or not,' he said with soft menace. 'I don't actually care. But just in case, I'm warning you. Harm anyone in my family, in any way whatsoever, and I'll turn you into mincemeat and feed you to my dogs.'

'Can't—' She grimaced and he let her go. 'Can't you take a ribbing any more?' she muttered, regretting her impulsive remarks. Darn! She'd have to coax him round now, before pumping him for information. 'I was only trying to keep this painfully awkward reunion on the light side. You didn't have to react like a Sicilian gangster with

a persecution complex. Come on, Julio! You're being ul-
tra-touchy,' she protested.

'Mmm. I'm a little preoccupied thinking about this
woman I'm pursuing,' he said softly. He gave a faint
smile. 'Pity she doesn't know how fiercely I will defend
my family,' he murmured. After a moment's thought, he
added, 'Remember when that prefect made a smutty remark about my sister?' He turned inscrutable eyes on her.

Randall nodded slowly. 'You knocked seven bells out
of him,' she said, nervously wondering where this was
leading.

'I meant to kill him,' came the stark reply.

Awed, Randall remembered his blind fury, the amazement of the other boys that anyone could lose his temper
with such spectacular results. It had been quite a sight,
bloodied arms and legs in the middle of an admiring circle
and two masters dragging away the tornado that was Julio.

'Everyone talked about it for weeks,' she said slowly.
'No one had seen an eleven-year-old try to take on half
the sixth form.'

'I have even more power to wield now,' he said enigmatically. 'Physical and influential—especially here, in
Andalucía, through my father's family connections.'

She looked blankly at him. It wasn't like Julio to boast.
Perhaps it was a threat. But the implications of what he'd
said were making her stomach churn. 'Your father was
from Andalucía?' she said in dismay. How would that
affect her work for Don Carlos? Would he know the
Quadra family? Her heart sank. She was to start in a few
days.

'Correct. And despite the fact that we visited rarely and
only my sister lives here, the Quadra name still has the
power to make things happen. I think you'll discover
that.'

Randall felt a shiver of apprehension. 'I don't understand.'

'You will.' He smiled coldly. 'Goodbye, Randall.'

Her eyes widened in surprise and she hastily jumped down from the wall. 'Goodbye!' she repeated indignantly. 'Is that it? Hello, you're sweating, goodbye?'

There was ice in the depths of his eyes. 'I've shovelled dirt for you,' he said coldly. 'What more do you want?'

'An apology?' she suggested haughtily.

And he winced. Their eyes locked in combat. She heard cicadas whirring close by, the click of hoe on stone from the fertile valley beyond and the deep lowing of a cow before he finally answered.

'Whistle for it. I'll be damned if I give you an apology,' he said abruptly. 'I have none to make.' Confident. Categorical. Without an ounce of guilt in his tone.

Randall was stunned. 'Oh, Julio!' she said, her voice reproachful and accusing. 'How can you say that?'

'Because I did what I thought best at the time. You seem to have ended up quite happy,' he said in a low growl, as if she had no right to be. 'You were singing earlier, despite the rain and the work you had to do.'

'I am happy, blissfully so—no thanks to you,' she replied, flicking back her hair defiantly.

There was a flash of steel in his secretive eyes before they became blank again and it dawned on her that the vitality that had marked him out as a boy had been extinguished. The hairs on the nape of her neck stood on end. What *had* happened to him? Nothing joyful, she realised, and her face softened with an involuntary compassion.

'Life's good to you,' he said in a sinister tone.

'Fabulous!' she enthused. 'Business *was* rotten and I haven't had two pennies to rub together,' she told him with utter frankness, 'but at last things are going well for me.'

'I see.' There was a pause. 'And you work…*here*?' he asked softly, the muscles in his jaw ominously clenched. 'In Ronda?'

Randall tensed. She must find out where he was staying and avoid that place like the plague. 'Torremolinos at the moment,' she explained, cautiously watching for some re-action. But his face was implacable. 'I maintain the gardens of some of the holiday complexes.' Thinking that soon—if she could avoid Julio and keep her new job—she might be able to give that work up, her face softened into a contented-cat smile. 'But that's all about to change.' Her eyes sparkled with excitement. 'I have,' she smiled, 'Great Expectations!'

'How nice,' he said politely, a politeness tinged with menace. 'What's the new job? Round here, is it?'

A sudden fear knotted up her insides. There was something not quite right about his interest. Randall studied him carefully and decided not to tell him anything more. An instinctive caution warned her not to trust his sudden fascination with the details of her life.

'I have to keep it a secret,' she said, deadpan, defending her privacy. 'My new boss said that if I told anyone I was teaching him to plant pansies he'd never live it down.'

'Very amusing,' drawled Julio, his eyes gleaming with suppressed annoyance. She beamed at him, enjoying the fact that he hated not to be told things. 'Your plans must be very special if you won't divulge them. You're quite ambitious, aren't you?' he mused, a chilling shrewdness tightening his mouth.

'*Very*,' she said emphatically. She had to be, with her darling Tom to provide for. He'd have the best, she thought fiercely. Her protection, her love, her devotion. 'I'm going to fly all the way to the top,' she said, exulting in her prospects. 'And get *filthy* rich.'

He nodded slowly. 'Yes. As I thought. You've become materialistic. I think I made the right decision in leaving you,' he drawled.

Randall's eyebrow lifted in disagreement. 'Right decision, wrong way of going about it,' she retorted proudly.

'The matter's dead and buried. Leave it,' he said irritably. 'You were told that I was unable to marry you. What more can be said?'

Randall fiercely blanked out what her reaction had been to the devastating news. 'I admit it was a *terribly* sweet letter from your lawyer.' Sarcasm. But how else could she prevent the upsurge of emotion that threatened to destroy her composure? 'I'm surprised you bothered to sit in his office and dictate it!' she muttered.

'I didn't. I left it to him,' said Julio shortly, his eyes bleak. 'I didn't want to see you again or to have any contact with you at all. I don't even know what he wrote.'

'That's ungentlemanly and cowardly.' It gave her some satisfaction to see his lips whiten at the blow to his honour. 'Let me tell you how it began. ''The Marquis sends his regrets''. Regrets!' she rasped shakily, reliving the heartstopping moment when she'd read those words. 'Regrets! As if you were turning down some casual tea-party instead of the woman you'd—you'd vowed you loved—'

'There's never an easy way,' he growled.

'Some methods create less hurt than others,' she husked. 'Yours took the prize for ruthlessness. Once you abandon a girl, you do it thoroughly, don't you? No looking back.'

'Looking back is fatal. How did you feel when you got the letter?' he asked harshly.

'Suicidal,' she grated, lifting her head proudly and giving him a hostile stare.

His eyes flickered. 'Not for long. You're alive,' he pointed out coldly.

'I—!' Randall was speechless with rage. She hastily clamped her mouth shut. Shortly before receiving the solicitor's letter, she'd been on the brink of telling Julio that she was pregnant. When he'd fled like a wolf in the night, the world had seemed a barren, inhospitable place. Only Tom had saved her sanity—and the need to find some way of coping with the daily worries of any unmarried mother without family, without money, without love…

Anger made her temper flare. 'I can't believe you can be so unemotional!' she seethed.

'I imagine that the detached tone of the letter—and my obvious indifference to your fate—made you hate me,' he suggested cynically, but she detected a probing note, almost as if he was keenly interested in her reaction to his callous departure.

'Hate? Oh, I think that's a little mild,' she said in glacial tones. 'Good grief, Julio! My mouth must have been still warm from your kisses when you married your wealthy countess, two weeks after walking out on me. *Two weeks*!' she seethed. 'Have you no concept of what you did? Are you completely amoral? How the devil do you *think* I felt?' she yelled.

He shrugged, his eyes quite blank. 'It's over,' he said infuriatingly, dismissing the anguish she'd suffered. It was as though she'd come down with a nasty attack of greenfly and nothing worse.

'My God!' she raged. 'How could I have imagined I loved you? I must have been blinded by your charm not to see that you were using me! No wonder some women turn against men and milk them for all they've got!'

There was a silence. She cringed at the frighteningly malevolent look on his face. 'Do they? Are you trying to tell me something, Randall?' he asked, coldly menacing. 'Do I detect a hint of female revenge being planned in that beautiful head?'

'Oh, the thought is tempting! Take it from me, I planned your death and destruction a thousand times,' she admitted grimly. 'Any woman would in the circumstances.'

His jaw clenched. 'Is that a fact?' he muttered.

'I can't bear this,' she muttered to herself. 'Once we were friends, as close as—'

'An acorn in its cup, I think I said,' he reminded her cruelly, his mouth twisted bitterly.

She winced. 'I can't believe we grew up together,' she said in a low voice. 'Shared so many things—'

'Forget the past!' he snarled savagely, making her jump with his vehemence. 'God! I wish I'd never set eyes on you!' he ground out.

Randall fought back a cry of anguish. Shaken, she looked at Julio with sorrowful eyes, trying to reconcile this unfeeling brute with the man who'd taught her how to live through her senses. 'We had some good times,' she faltered in protest.

He didn't answer. But there was something in his smouldering look that made her catch her breath. From the whitewashed houses of Ronda came the idle chords of a distant guitar. It punctuated the heavy silence between them with the sound of haunting gypsy music which never failed to thrill her and stir every bone in her body.

And as she stood there with the sun's warmth on her upturned face, hearing the rushing water and over-whelmed by the perfumed oils from the aromatic herbs, she felt a breeze ruffling her hair, sending the silky golden strands gliding across her face. She saw Julio's shadowed eyes flicker in recognition and knew instinctively that he'd remembered one day in the orchard when he'd spread her hair over the primroses and slowly, sensually, roped her body with a daisy chain.

'Yes. Good times,' he said huskily.

She was breathing heavily, pushing the heart-stopping moments away. Memories, a heightened awareness and an illegitimate child had been his only legacies to her, and for those she could almost forgive him. Almost.

'And that's all it was, for you, wasn't it? A bit of fun. I had no idea at the time that I'd meant so little to you,' she said, amazed that she could speak so normally to him.

'Try not to pout so often,' he said sardonically. 'It's very provocative. I have some advice which you'd do well to heed. Steer clear of married men, forget any ideas of vengeance and you'll come to no harm. *Claro*?'

'Ye-e-es,' she said slowly, blinking up at him in some puzzlement. 'But I want to know—'

'Goodbye, Randall,' he growled, angling his hat deep over his forehead. Snapping his fingers at the grazing stallion, he strode purposefully towards it as if eager to put the past safely back in a sealed box again. The Marquis sends his regrets...

She stared after him, her face pale with worry and anger, torn between a dignified, casual farewell and running to him, screaming questions.

Where was he staying? Where would he be working? What danger was there of them meeting, she holding Tom's hand... Oh, God, she whimpered inwardly. She *had* to know. Or she'd spend the next few weeks petrified with fear every time she and Tom were together. Julio had spoken of vengeance. What would he do to her, what awful fury would grip him and be unleashed on her head, if he knew that she'd kept the existence of his son from him?

CHAPTER TWO

FOR a few moments, Randall was paralysed with fear. Julio's horse whinnied and pawed the ground, tossing its head so that the long black mane flicked into the air. Swifts and scimitar-winged swallows swooped over them all in an acrobatic ballet. Her agitation increased when her brain steadfastly refused to send the right messages to her leaden legs.

She saw the stallion arch its neck when Julio affectionately touched the glossy mane, his fingers lingering on the thick lustrous hairs. Then, as if unable to resist the temptation, he reached out to stroke the gleaming coat, as gently as if he were caressing a woman's skin.

To Randall's dismay, the quiver of response in the stallion was echoed by a tremor in her own body. Whether she wanted them or not, deeply sensual feelings were awakening in her, sending scurries of sensation chasing over her skin as she mentally, oh, and physically and emotionally too, transferred Julio's lightly skimming fingertips to the long-neglected curves of her own body.

'Please, Julio!' she husked, and had to moisten her dry lips because there was no way she could speak any more, and she didn't know if that was due to fear, need, or horror that her sexual craving for Julio was still buried inside her. Correction: was being resurrected with devastating effect on her highly developed sense of decency.

With a start, she became aware that he was looking back at her, slanting her a savage, almost voracious glance from under his brows that captured her as surely as if he'd tied her with a rope. 'You want something, Randall?' he asked thickly.

30

'Yes... I—want—don't go...' The lump of dread
blocked her throat still. She tried to smile, to be bright
and detached, but nothing happened and he vaulted into
the saddle effortlessly. *'Stay, please!'* she cried in panic,
just to keep him from leaving. He mustn't go. She had to
be sure that she and Tom could walk around safely.
'Stay,' she begged, dry-mouthed and husky.

And then realised how he'd interpreted that low cry. A
desire blazed in his eyes that wasn't sexually driven or
even born of a healthy male lust. It was violent and predatory as if he wanted to hurt her physically, to tear her
apart with his bare hands and throw the pieces into the
ravine, and it struck her dumb with its sheer malevolence.

He turned his horse and came slowly towards her, the
brief display of anger gone. Or it had been successfully
masked. She wasn't quite sure and that was very unnerving. Instead, he projected a mocking self-assurance as
though she'd confirmed his worst doubts about her—and
meant to collect.

Warily, Randall moved backwards. His eyes upon her,
taunting her with a triumphant arrogance, he urged the
stallion gently after her. Till she felt grass beneath her
feet and then the coolness of shade and the rough bark of
a tree against her back.

'You want me to stay?' he asked throatily.

Infuriatingly, nothing came out of her mouth, only the
shape of the words. His mouth twisted into a cynical smile
and she finally forced the words out in a harsh explosion.
'I only wanted to—'

'To do what?' Julio asked softly. 'Relive old times?
Tumble in the grass? Swim naked in the river?' He leaned
forward in the saddle, his eyes drowsy in contemplation
of her upturned face, luminously pale in the shadows of
the twisting olive tree.

'Don't, Julio,' she muttered, washed with sensation. He
let a silence surround them and bind them together.
Around her the cistus poured its oils into the air and the

sound of bees all but drowned distant echoes of hollow goat-bells in the pasturelands. Everything conspired to torture her and made her mouth bitter.

'We have everything, here,' he said huskily. 'All the beautiful senses combined. Smell the lavender? I could crush it between my fingers and transfer its oils to every inch of your body. There's rosemary; a sprig would scent your hair...*all* your hair,' he reminded her ruthlessly, his eyes dropping with shaming insolence to where the heat coiled and burned in her, where muscles tightened with every powerful sensory memory he conjured up.

Randall shook her head in silent protest. And fought her way out of her trance by digging her nails into her palms till it hurt. 'My goodness! We were impressively in advance of the natural beauty shops,' she joked shakily. 'Did we really do all that?' And she could have groaned when her body leapt at the thought of Julio's exploring fingers, dipping into its curves and crevices...

'And more,' he said thickly.

The sultry air between them shimmered, making Randall feel dizzy. Or was it that she could hardly breathe? The hard work had robbed her lungs of air...of course. Her nails did their job again. For Tom's sake, she couldn't let herself weaken.

'Would you mind backing off?' she asked with a sweet smile that wavered at the edges. 'I'm wary of horses. And it's rolling its eyes at me. Give me space. I only wanted to ask—'

'You don't want sex?' he asked baldly. 'It looked as if you were offering.'

Her jaw dropped open and then she remembered not to pout and get accused of provoking him. 'Is it your policy to insult every woman you meet, or is it just me?' she asked through her teeth, feeling that steam might come out of her ears any moment.

'Only you.' He smiled mockingly when a flash of anger animated her face. 'I remember how eager you were, you see,' he added, a warm smouldering making lights in his eyes gleam at her. 'Desperate—even for our first kiss. I always wondered how much of an accident it was, when we tumbled down that bank of daisies like young puppies, and ended up in a heap of tangled arms and legs, laughing.' His words became caresses, as though he were reaching out to touch her with them.

He was scoring a direct hit. She hoped he didn't know. 'What rollicking innocent fun,' she said calmly. Or it would have been calm, if it hadn't been for that small give-away tremor throughout.

'It was a little more than that, by your reaction at the time. When I kissed you,' he murmured softly, holding her luminous eyes with his relentless stare, 'you—virtually—*melted*.'

He punched each word at her softly, the impact of his husky, erotic voice hitting her in the solar plexus and taking her breath away. It wasn't fair, she thought, momentarily defenceless. She'd loved him; she'd been waiting and waiting for him to kiss her—and, when he had, her emotions had overflowed because the world had stood still and then whirled her into womanhood, arousing all her deepest emotions.

Desperate to stay ice-cool, she lifted a sardonic eyebrow. 'Don't say you've been kidding yourself it was your technique!' she mocked. 'Everyone knows that I tend to throw myself enthusiastically into whatever I do,' she continued, worried that she was letting herself get diverted again and appalled by the deep hoarseness of her voice. She tried to stiffen her wobbly lower lip and felt her body contract when his hot eyes scorched imaginary kisses on her soft mouth. 'Kissing is one of many things I like.' She groaned. She'd meant that to sound casual. It had come out as if she was man-mad. 'Like chips,' she said crushingly. 'Nice—'

'Nice?' he murmured, still contemplating her mouth.

'How you English understate the case! Randall, we both know that it was total and complete surrender.'

Insolent brute! she seethed. 'Young love is so over-the-top,' she said, giving a dismissive shrug of her slender shoulders. 'I was awfully innocent. Completely ignorant of men and how easily they're aroused. Your reaction was alarming.' For alarming, she thought miserably, read wonderful. He'd been tender, full of awe and hesitant adoration. It had been the nearest she'd ever come to feeling like a goddess on earth. She shut her mind to that. 'Not very polite of you to remind me,' she chided with a reproving wag of her finger. 'Now, about where—?'

'Do you still over-react?' he asked silkily.

'That's for me to know and you to wonder about,' she fended him off, stiffening warily. There were messages in the drowsy eyes and she sensed a more urgent danger facing her, apparent in Julio's extravagantly sensual mouth and the sexual menace in his body. She tried to make herself even flatter against the tree.

'It's a beautiful day,' he said in a low, throbbing murmur. 'Perfect for us to lie on the grass and explore one another again, slowly, with infinite attention to detail. I could drive you crazy, Randall,' he whispered, his eyes dark and fathomless. 'Torment you with pleasure. Scorch your body with heat, inside and out.'

Randall clenched her teeth against the thudding urgency of her pulses, her body washed with the husky lure of Julio's softly insistent voice. 'You're trying it on,' she said flatly. 'I'm sure you're aware that someone you know could come by.'

He didn't deny that. Or agree. 'Perhaps a long, leisurely afternoon of sex in the open air might ease our…tense feelings about each other,' he suggested in a muted growl and she thought miserably, Yes. Yes, it would.

'So would murder,' she retorted instead, sheer self-preservation keeping her apparently calm. 'Is that an option I can take up?'

The corner of his mouth twitched. 'Why go that far? Sex has the effect of releasing violent and obsessive emotions—and carries fewer consequences,' he drawled.

Randall bit back a meaningful 'Huh!' It hadn't for her. 'I know,' she said smugly, to annoy him. 'But unfortunately for your plans to fill a long, leisurely afternoon, I gave up sex with upper-class rats long ago.'

'Did you, I wonder?' His dark brow arched in disbelief. 'I'm all in favour of you taking what pleasure you can, where you can.' His nostrils curled in distaste. 'But within reason.'

'And that's what you did with me—take your pleasure?' she asked huskily.

His expression was cold and calculating and it chilled her bones. 'Of course,' he answered.

Randall was shocked to hear him admit that she'd been one of the pleasures he'd enjoyed. Like roast lamb and chocolate éclairs, she thought, deeply upset.

In Andalucía, which he carried in his blood, life was black or white, hot or cold, always extremes. And women were traditionally classified as whores or madonnas. It was now perfectly clear what had happened at Broadfield. To Julio, who was used to accepting that well-bred women were taboo, she'd been a fun trip on a Ferris wheel. Ready for a whirl whenever he wanted to switch on the mechanism. Eager, willing… She blushed. His remarks had made her feel like a toy he'd take out of the cupboard and discarded when boredom set in. *Swine*!

Tom wouldn't grow up with such bigoted beliefs; she'd make sure of that—and now she was even more determined Julio would never ruin her son with his chauvinism. She smiled absently, thinking of the noisy, crazy breakfast they'd had that morning. They'd hastily cooked a rather hefty tortilla for him to take to nursery school to go with his *molletes* and their faces had been splattered in beaten egg from Tom's enthusiastic efforts.

Julio let out an impatient grunt and she came out of her

reverie to find that he was eyeing her with a jaundiced
look. 'Forgive me for interrupting your no doubt delight-
ful recollections of your activities last night,' he drawled
lazily, 'but would you tell me what you want so I can
leave before Christmas is upon us?'

She flushed. 'OK. I will. Where are you staying?' she
asked with blinding directness. Tasmania would be nice.
Hell, one step better.

The black, unfathomable eyes flickered and stayed
guarded. 'Various places. Why?' he asked suspiciously.

It wasn't good enough! she wailed inside. Details, she
wanted details! 'Because,' she said, wanting to defend her
apparent desire to know his every movement, 'it may surprise you to know, but I'm not ecstatic about bumping
into you again. You remind me of things I'd rather forget.'

'Lavender rubs?' he enquired lazily.

'Crying,' she countered, to throw him off balance, and
watched him mentally counting to ten as he always used
to when incensed beyond reason. 'Howling my eyes out,
night after night.' The big shoulders sank back into place
from where they had risen, his anger ruthlessly under control. 'So you see why I want to avoid you,' she continued,
hammering the point home.

A hand resting nonchalantly on the high pommel of his
tooled leather saddle, he flicked her such a look of disdain
down the length of his Brando nose that she cringed back
against the tree. 'I can't think why you imagine we'll
bump into one another,' he said cuttingly. 'Surely we in-
habit totally different worlds?'

Randall's stomach knotted. The doubt of her own worth
returned again, this time with a vengeance, all those de-
structive feelings of inferiority that had begun towards the
end of their time together at Broadfield School when jealous under-matrons had pointed out how unsuitable she
was for Julio. And his rejection had confirmed that. The
matrons had laughed at her then. Laughed and called her
a fool, adding to her humiliation and misery.

'I get around,' she stated flatly. 'If you're staying near we might meet and—'

'Can you *possibly* know people in my social circle?' he wondered softly, and it seemed for a moment that there was a hint of menace behind the question.

She dismissed this thought, managed to laugh and indicated her work clothes. 'Hob-nobbing with the aristos?' she cried brightly. 'Does it look as if I'm on their guest list?!' She remembered Santini and her expression gentled. 'Though…I do know a really *nice* grandee. He's an absolute poppet.'

His face became grim, as if she had no business to breathe the same air. 'You know this man socially?'

Her eyes danced in wry amusement. 'Not exactly!'

'So I won't be meeting you at a party or a reception. Perhaps on a landing, then?'

'You've lost me,' she said with a small, uncertain laugh.

'A bedroom landing?' he prompted cynically.

The vicious gibe made her blink. Hastily she sharpened up a few weapons to defend herself again and resisted the urge to knock him off his horse with her shovel. 'I gather you're suggesting that I'm unsuitable for cocktails, but fine for Horlicks and bathtime frolics.'

His mouth twitched. 'Something like that.'

'Pity the feminist movement hasn't impinged on your conscious mind,' she sighed. 'I think it would be rather amusing,' she mused, 'if we peasant girls decided to turn the tables on you upper-class chauvinists. I'm sure,' she murmured, longing to provoke him, 'I could make a lucrative career out of bewitching an arrogant grandee if I wanted to.' She slanted her eyes at him in defiance, ruthlessly crushing her inner pain.

'If that's even a half-serious suggestion,' he said in an icy drawl, 'I would advise you to forget it. If you want to make a career out of whoring, stick to whatever men you've already got panting at your door. Tangle with the cream of Spanish manhood and you'll find yourself floundering out of your depth.'

Over and over again he was drumming it into her that she wasn't good enough for him or his peers and she kept wanting to yell that she was. 'You'd win medals in snobbery, Julio,' she declared irritably. 'I think there's been a social revolution since you were here,' she pointed out.

'Don't you believe it,' he said cynically. 'Deep down, things are the same as they always were. Spanish men enjoy flirting and having as many affairs as they can get away with.' His eyes glittered. 'If a man's been starved of food, he grabs what's going.'

'Meaning?' she muttered.

'You know the moral code here. It's very strict, very hard on sexually active men,' he murmured. 'As a young, hungry male brought up in Buenos Aires by the codes of Andalucía, I remember I found it very tantalising being denied access to women. A bitter-sweet torment. Frustration is so exciting, don't you think? It ensures that we think of sex all day long.' His voice became husky. 'Every moment of our waking hours.'

The warm, indolent look in his eyes made her stomach coil with nerves. It told her that he was starving. Thinking about sex. Wanting physical release. And he knew that she'd once been willing and eager. Why not again? he was thinking, by the predatory expression on his face. Once tarnished...

'A waste of good brain, thinking about sex all the time,' she suggested, trying to break the sexual tension thickening the air between them and slowing her tongue. 'Besides, it must make calculating your bar bills difficult.'

His mouth quirked. 'That's why we try to feed our hunger as often as possible, wherever possible. Deny a man something and he'll want it,' murmured Julio, his sensual voice sliding like silk into her weakening body. His eyes darkened to an inky black. Randall tried to look away but she couldn't. Miserably she knew he was an aphrodisiac to her. I want you, his eyes said. Without strings.

'Give it to him and he won't?' she said apprehensively, seeing where his thoughts were leading.

He smiled faintly. 'You're getting the picture. I'm sure you know that a rampant male with sex uppermost in his mind will promise a woman anything to get her to bed.'

'Oh, yes. It happened to me, didn't it? You were going to marry me. Once bitten, twice shy,' she said coldly. 'In future I mean to get contracts drawn up first.'

'You're showing a remarkable sense of self-preservation,' he drawled. 'I hope you've taken on board the fact that an affair with a high-class Spaniard has absolutely no future. We don't respect women who easily surrender their virtue. And marriage is out of the question.'

The colour of dark roses stained her cheeks. He was explaining why he'd jilted her. He wasn't going to marry a woman he could sleep with before the ceremony. Wasn't he supposed to exercise any self-control too? She quivered with rage. 'I know,' she grated. 'The rules are carved on my heart.'

'Then stay away from your *nice* grandee,' he snapped.

'Do what? Like hell I will!' she cried indignantly. 'You're not interfering in that arrangement! I've got there by my own determination and if I want to be upwardly mobile then I darn well will be, you—you self-opinionated, class-conscious bigot!'

'If that's the attitude you're taking, then suffer the consequences, you stupid little fool!' he muttered savagely and gathered the stallion beneath him, preparing to go.

'No, wait!' she wailed. 'I haven't...' With a sudden panicky rush, she launched herself forwards and grabbed Julio's soft leather boot at the ankle just as it lifted to kick the horse into a canter.

'*No!* Randall!' he snarled in fury.

'You never answered me properly!' she cried, her eyes

almost silvered as they blazed into his. Begging him was deeply humiliating, but she'd sit in a pit of snakes for Tom. 'You have to tell me,' she insisted despairingly. 'Where exactly are you staying?'

He stilled the skittering horse with a barked command and a crushing pressure of his thighs. 'You must be desperate to know!' he observed shrewdly. 'Are you afraid I'll find out your secret?' She blanched in dismay, but before she could make any denial the impatient stallion deliberately knocked Randall off-balance. '*Watch out*!' rasped Julio.

In a split-second reaction, he bent in the saddle and grabbed her roughly before she could fall on to the hard cobbles. One strong arm swept her off her feet and for a moment she hung suspended in mid-air while his horse snapped irritably in her direction. Then she had been drawn up out of harm's reach and deposited firmly across Julio's warm, hard thighs.

Out of harm's reach? She smelt his unmistakable fragrance: subtle exotic scents from the Orient and more pagan ones of unadulterated male. Beneath her left hand she could feel the stallion's hot satin coat and the hard muscle under it. It mirrored the sensation under her right palm: the soft luxury of smooth grey cloth sheathing the iron of Julio's powerful bicep.

Wide-eyed and breathless, she felt her breasts do a little shimmy as the predatory hunger in Julio's eyes and the sinfulness of his mouth reached into her body and filled it with an echoing need.

'Please…' She blinked helplessly, wondering where her voice had gone. She wanted to be put down, *quickly*, before she flung her arms around his neck to feed her starving mouth. She tried again. 'Would you—?'

'*Damn* you, Randall!' he growled, his huge hands crushing her arms. 'Why did you call me back? Why couldn't you leave well alone?'

Her instinctive reaction was to push on his shoulders

to open the space between them. Her body strained away from him and her head tipped back so that her hair flowed untrammelled in a rippling, golden sheet. She felt the stretch of her T-shirt across her breasts and then a sudden shocking warmth; the hard thrust of male virility where his pelvis pressed against her hip.

'Julio!' she gasped in shock. 'You're...!'

'Sure I am. Is it any wonder, the way you've been throwing your body around?' he asked sardonically.

Ruthlessly he hauled her close to him again, his harsh breath rasping unevenly on her face and warming a path into the sensitive recesses of her opened mouth. Tantalising. Intoxicating. And weakness stole over her at the pressure of his firm hand on her naked thigh, each fingertip gently rotating.

With dismay, she could feel the taut peaks of her breasts pressing into his chest as if they had no shame at all, saying 'please' more powerfully, more emphatically than she could have ever dreamed, and she let out a muted mutter to deny her body's betrayal.

'*Madre de Dios*!' he whispered softly under his breath.

She gulped, sensing with a numbed realisation that his anger had changed to something far more dangerous. She was in his arms and giving out signals like a pulsating glow-worm signalling to its mate and, in his hunger, he'd grab what was on the menu for today and devour her alive.

'Put—me—down!' she said raggedly, her eyes glued wistfully to his arching, infinitely kissable mouth.

But her body was double-crossing her by the drooping of her lids, the feebleness of her rejection and the terrible awakening of her body after years of abstinence. It didn't know that Julio was married. Only her mind did, and that seemed incapable of controlling the overpowering urge to yield without a fight.

She could have wept with shame. He couldn't mistake the fact that she was willing. Available. The most brazen of women. Easy virtue. A sob rasped in her throat. It sounded like a sigh.

'You respond so beautifully,' he husked, his dark eyes velvet with languorous sexuality. His finger flickered over her sulky mouth in wonder. 'No inhibitions. Like a little animal.'

'No, I'm not,' she breathed, her mouth dry as he worked her body into his.

He smiled. 'Pouting again...' Gently he drew his nail along the bow of her parted lips and then tested their swelling softness, drawing a shuddering sigh of despair from deep inside her. His smile vanished and he looked suddenly cruel. 'Is it more exciting with married men?' he said through clenched teeth. And he let his hand slide to her throat, where it pressed against her windpipe.

'No! No, no, no, *no*!' she whispered, desperately wriggling. Hampered by his arms and her slowly responding limbs, the movement turned into a sensual undulation that caused Julio to draw in his breath and lower his hand to rest against the deep valley of her breasts. 'No,' she mumbled in abject misery, cringing from his touch.

He laughed softly and she knew he'd take no notice of her. Julio had been indulged from the cradle. He didn't even respect her. 'Sure about that? Let's explore the hypothesis,' he murmured.

Rigid with horror, she watched his face come closer and fill her vision, felt his mouth claim hers, move over her lips with a heart-rending memory of sweet loving, summer days, warm grass, starlit nights...

Someone moaned, low and husky, and she found that she was clutching Julio's shoulders, on the brink of returning his kiss, seduced by her own poignant memories. With an effort, she dragged open her eyes, forcing herself to resist, struggling ineffectually and wondering with mounting panic how she could escape unharmed.

Julio's lashes lay thick and alluring on his high cheekbones and yet, as if he knew everything she did, they fluttered up and he watched her inner struggle with mocking eyes while he crushed her mouth beneath his in a calculated show of strength that contrasted with the tantalisingly delicate caress of his fingers on her bare thigh. His teeth began gently to savage her jawline.

'Let me go,' she said in a low, trembling voice. 'Don't make me wish you in hell again...' If she'd ever harboured illusions about Julio, they were shattered now. Brutally. Her tears began to flow, trickling down her cheeks.

Then to the corner of her mouth. Where he tasted the salt there, tensed and slowly drew back, an unreadable expression on his face. 'I hope those are real,' he grated.

To her astonishment, she found herself being pushed off the saddle and guided to the ground. For a moment, blinking back her tears, she swayed, was steadied. Julio appeared to be completely in control of himself and she envied him.

It felt as though she'd been tossed into the gorge and swept along by a torrent. Her bruised mouth throbbed— but it wasn't sated. Shamefully wanton, she ached to be kissed till nightfall and through to the next full moon. And couldn't believe she could harbour such covetous feelings towards another woman's husband or that she could hate him so fervently.

'Lecher!' she grated, dashing the back of her hand impatiently across her eyes and desperate to let out the strangled sobs inside her. But too proud. 'Adulterer!' she flung wildly.

'Ditto,' he drawled.

Her eyes blazed a denial but he was almost right. She'd betrayed herself, all her principles. 'No. I won't take the blame for what happened!' she flared. 'You've been waiting for a chance to manhandle me ever since you complained about my provocative clothes. I never thought you'd treat me like a whore, Julio. Why did you? To hurt me? To make me learn my place? Perhaps to prove to yourself that I'm a tramp and you were justified in ditching me? *Why?*'

'Why?' he snarled. 'You know damn well. You're a slut and soon it'll be common knowledge. Look into your conscience and answer your own damn question.' Her head snapped up in a defiant reaction so that her hair swirled around her flushed face. Julio's upper lip curled in contempt. 'God, woman, get a mirror and check yourself out. You're still fired up and ready to go!'

Her jaw dropped open. 'I'm *what?*' she spluttered in fury.

In answer, the back of his hand brushed over her firm breasts. She felt the cushiony give of their soft swell against the relentless pressure of his knuckles, then the quivering hardness of each springing nipple begging with a humiliating brazen eagerness for a repeat of his caress. Her mortified eyes met his mocking, confident gaze and she knew with a sickening sensation that she'd instantly proved his theory. Women enticed. Men, poor lambs, were helpless.

'You ask for trouble with every breath you take,' he scathed. 'Carry on as you are, and I'll make damn sure you'll get it.'

'*Ohhh!*' she growled in sheer exasperation and stumbled back out of his reach, half hysterical with rage. 'I didn't want you—'

'Spare me the denial.' He'd cut across her half-truth with venomous ferocity. 'You think I can't read women by now? I suggest you put a temporary hold on the heaving breasts and wet T-shirt,' he sneered.

'Yes, sir!' she snapped. 'I'll make a request for the rain to stop when I'm shovelling topsoil in future and I'll try not to breathe when I exert myself,' she added angrily. 'And what do you suggest I wear? A packing case and a paper bag on my head?'

'Watch your tongue,' he said softly. 'And keep it tucked primly in that enticing mouth. I wondered what kind of woman you'd become. Now I know. You don't care if a man's married or not, do you?'

'I—' she croaked.

'You disgust me,' he growled. 'I'm warning you to lay off. Do you understand? Or I will hurt you so badly that you'll never be able to make love again, on horseback, in bed or,' he said, his face livid with anger, 'even in a valley of meadow flowers. *Claro*?' he roared.

Oh, God! she thought, pained by the memory. 'You cruel *louse*!' she said shakily. 'And no, it isn't clear. I don't know what you're—'

But he'd driven his heels sharply into his horse's flanks before she could continue her protest, cry out, storm at him or invite him down to relieve the miserable ache inside her. She didn't know what she wanted, only that he'd left her utterly confused—and nursing resentfully the knowledge that his touch had aroused and excited her.

But, worst of all, she still had no idea where he was staying nor how to avoid bumping into him again. Julio's systematic and deliberate humiliation, the shame of knowing he was aware of her physical attraction for him, the painful memories—all of those she'd been forced to undergo. And for *nothing*. Randall let out a long, despairing moan.

'Oh, rot in hell, Julio Valdez!' she yelled, and kicked her back tyre hard in frustrated temper. Miserably she glowered at the foaming River Guadalévin, following where it ribboned in extravagant silvery curves through the green fields and olive groves. She hurled a stone with all her strength and it fell into the water, disappearing without a trace.

'Goodbye, Julio,' she said bitterly. And her eyes filled with tears for the idyllic childhood they'd spent together. It was more than dead and buried. It had been hung, drawn and quartered over the last hour or so and with all her heart she hoped that she'd never see Julio ever again.

She must turn her energies to protecting Tom. All the

misery and humiliation she'd experienced whenever she'd crossed Julio's path would be nothing compared with the agonies she'd feel if Julio ever got near her son and tried to claim him.

A hardness slowly crept into her. She'd defend her child like a tigress. Tooth and claw. Maybe she and Tom didn't have much by some standards, but they were happy together and Julio wouldn't destroy that. Anxiety gnawing at her insides, she forced herself to drive on up the hill. Her body was shaking so much that it felt as if she'd just cut a lawn on her knees with a pair of nail scissors.

Eventually she dumped the topsoil—in the right place this time—and took a long, circuitous route to her yard in Torremolinos, just in case she was being followed. Ridiculous, yes, but Julio was wealthy enough to employ people to do his dirty work for him and it was a risk she couldn't take. Pray God he never traced her.

Hot, bothered and late, she found herself stuck in a monumental traffic jam on the coast road. Amid the stench of petrol fumes, thick cloying dust and a gaudy forest of advertising signs, she waited impatiently, coldly suffering the inevitable chat-up lines and barracking from the men around her.

Dissatisfied with her handling of the meeting with Julio, she went through the clever, sophisticated things she could have dazzled him with and tried her best not to think about the bittersweet past. But her surroundings seemed to be determined to remind her. The dying palms and eucalpytus trees, surrendering to the relentless traffic pollution, made her think of the garden at Broadfield School.

A stab of anguish thrust through her heart like the steel prongs of a fork. She and Julio had spent years creating the garden. Under her beloved father's guidance, they'd filled it with plants to arouse the senses. Trees with tex-tured bark, graceful willows and heady lilies, apple mint, soft fruit, plants with rustling leaves and exploding seed pods.

It had been their shared Paradise. The kind of garden Tom would love. Her face softened with motherly love. Julio wouldn't spoil her future as he'd spoiled her past. Tom would have that garden when she'd achieved her ambitions—with the help of Don Carlos.

Yes. She was lucky. She had Tom. And she meant to keep him.

That evening, when she kissed her handsome son goodnight, she watched his smudge-dark eyes slowly close and the thick black lashes flutter then become still. Tom had Julio's strong bones, his breathtaking beauty. A way of looking from under a forest of thick black lashes that stopped her heart.

She loved him intensely. He'd been her whole world from the moment he'd first moved within her and she had wonderingly placed her hand on her stomach where the gentle flutter had miraculously made her stop moping about Julio and start thinking of her unborn child's welfare. And now Tom could be in danger.

'Oh, God!' she groaned.

Her fists clenched as she fought back the stomach-churning panic. This was the old Spain, where men ruled with a benevolent, adoring dictatorship, where they were all-powerful. Perhaps it was wonderfully protective for women and bliss to be cherished, honoured and respected. But a man's claim to his son was unquestioned and a son was evidence of a man's virility. A son brought pride to his father's face. And continued the bloodline.

'They'd take my son...'

She pushed her knuckles into her mouth to stop the wail that would have woken Tom. She was not respectable—that was her fear. She was an unmarried mother and a foreigner. Was that why Julio was trying to blacken her reputation? To suggest she was a whore? To sow the first seeds...

Randall frowned, impatient with her wild thoughts. She'd decided earlier that if he knew already that she had a child he would surely have forced her to reveal where she lived. Perhaps Julio had children by Elvira. That was why aristocrats married, to have heirs. Would he want Tom as well? His first-born... Her breath shuddered in sharply. Of course he would. And he'd get him.

She felt weak with a helpless dread. 'Tom, darling,' she whispered, burying her face into his warm neck. 'Oh, Tom!'

He stirred, and in his sleep his small hand rested on her head as if in comfort. Randall smiled through her tears and steadied herself. She and Julio wouldn't cross paths again. He'd never know she had a child. He mustn't.

CHAPTER THREE

SCRAPING away furiously at an encrusted lasagne dish and putting it to drain a little later, Randall looked out of the tiny caravan window at the soulless yard and knew that she'd do anything, anything to keep Tom safe, to ensure he never grew up to be like his callous, arrogant father who'd put duty and dynasty at the top of his list.

Tom, she was determined, would respect people for what they were, no matter what their walk of life, and he'd *never* use women or hurt them. She couldn't bear it if her son grew up to look down on her because she had little education and a poor background, nor if he treated women as ruthlessly as his father.

For the next couple of weeks, she realised that she'd be constantly looking over her shoulder, terrified that Julio would appear—perhaps to follow her and find out where she lived. She'd need to take precautions—elaborate ways home, a bit of backtracking. She shuddered at the thought of life without Tom and dismissed it immediately. It would be unbearable.

Wide-awake on the narrow convertible bed in the caravan, her eyes staring up at the discoloured ceiling, Randall thought about the awful meeting with Julio and wished fervently that it had never taken place. He'd been determined to humiliate her and prove that he'd been right to jilt her. She hadn't behaved much better. He'd belittled her and she'd spat bullets back.

'Mama!'

Her head jerked around and she saw her son sitting up in bed, looking at her with Julio's dark eyes. 'What is it, darling?' she said softly, swinging her legs down to the floor and slipping over to sit on his bed.

'You're sad. I like you happy,' he said anxiously. 'Be happy for me!'

She blinked at the command and momentarily felt a twinge of fear that Tom carried the haughty Quadra genes inside his five-year-old body. 'Men order, women obey', was the local saying. But then she saw his concern, smiled and hugged him.

'I am happy,' she said lightly.

Even as she reassured Tom, she knew that she wasn't as happy as she'd been as a teenager when her friendship with Julio had slowly grown into love. Nor was she as happy as she'd been earlier that day, before Julio had helped her to shovel soil from the cobbled lane.

Clouds were lining up on her horizon. They were threatening enough to cause a deluge if they emptied on her.

Tom's strong arms wrapped around her neck. 'I wish we had a daddy,' he whispered confidingly in her ear.

Her whole body tensed in shocked dismay. He'd never been bothered before! They'd been utterly self-sufficient. Stifling a cry for his sake, Randall gently moved back and studied her son's solemn face, seeing already that he would grow up to be the image of his father, and a mixture of pride and sorrow came with that realisation.

'Why, sweetheart?' she asked gently.

Tom smiled and her heart turned over. Julio's smile. 'Then he could work and bring us money to add to yours, so we can stay for always in Spain.'

'You like it here, don't you?' she said, pleased. Steve, her ex-tutor at her evening classes, had coaxed them to Spain and offered her a job when she'd been unemployed for a year. She bit her lip. She hadn't given a thought to Julio ever turning up, not when she knew his home was in Argentina with his heiress wife.

'It's smashing! I don't ever want us to leave. But a

daddy could give me cuddles when you're busy and make you happy and throw me in the air—'

'I can throw you in the air!' she protested, a little hurt. She'd taught him to play football, climb trees…

'Not as high,' he said earnestly. 'Not enough to make the wind rush round your face. We needn't keep the daddy for long. When I grow up I'll be your daddy and we can send him away.'

Randall laughed. 'Oh, Tom! It doesn't work like that! Daddies stay forever, just like mummies!'

'Ours didn't,' he said with inescapable truth. 'That wasn't very kind, was it?'

'No.' She steadied her voice. 'Never mind. I do love you!' she said, and cuddled him, incapable of saying any more because of the lump in her throat.

Settling him down again, she mused that Julio might be rich and powerful, but somehow she sensed that he'd ended up with less than she had—and she wouldn't swap for a billion pounds. Quietly she turned down Tom's night-light and tiptoed out.

Twinges of guilt still troubled her, however. Wilfully she'd denied Julio the joy—and the right—to know his son. She sighed. Even if he found out and didn't try to take her son from her, he'd almost certainly expect to lay down the law about his own son's education and upbringing.

Maybe Tom *could* benefit by growing up under Julio's protective wing. But, she sighed, that would mean he'd learn to put duty before warm, human emotion. Her face grew fierce. That she would never allow. Not in a million years.

Julio's contempt for her didn't matter, nor did his opinions. Not when she could measure her happiness by the love that shone in Tom's eyes. That was enough to make her world complete. The knowledge calmed her. And she'd always known she was richer than most people in having a son like Tom. Gradually her eyes closed, her problems more in perspective. She'd cope. Julio's presence in Spain was temporary, after all.

Bouncing back to her usual cheerful self again in the morning, she telephoned Steve to tell him of her change of fortune. But he was preoccupied with the illness of a close friend and was waiting for a call, so after making a few hasty arrangements she promised to give more details later.

Then she asked her friend Ana to collect Tom from nursery school and took her belongings some ten miles beyond Ronda to the cottage Don Carlos had pointed out from an upstairs window of his villa.

Here, she'd be safe. She and Tom could hide away for a while. She surveyed the low whitewashed building, its orange hooped tiles and the roses smothering it, and felt a sense of security.

'It's absolutely lovely,' she breathed, her eyes alight with pleasure. 'Oh, and a *garden*!' Tom would be *wild* about having space to run and play, instead of the ugly yard!

Her arms laden with the carrier bags she'd carried through the back garden gate, she waggled her fingers awkwardly towards the key in her pocket, planning to pick Tom up early and show him his new home. She couldn't *wait*.

'Hello, Randall. Been shopping?'

Julio. Behind her. She closed her eyes and felt the life drain out of her. 'I don't believe it!' she whispered, appalled.

Weakly she leaned forward till her forehead touched the hot wood of the door, all the excitement and delight in her new home wiped clean away. He'd been following her! For how long? And...had he seen her deliver Tom to the nursery? Slowly she turned, her eyes clouded, accusing pools of blue.

'Believe it now?' he mocked. She nodded dumbly,

waiting for him to denounce her. 'Ask me in,' he ordered lazily, his dark eyes raking her halter top and flowing cotton skirt. 'I like the juggling bears. That one,' he said, touching the ecstatically drunken bear on the high swell above her heart, 'is particularly cute.'

'Really?' she squeaked, and shrank back in case he investigated each one in turn. There were some in places, she saw, following his fascinated eyes, that lay half-hidden in the folds of the alarmingly revealing top. With remarkable presence of mind, she lifted one load of bags and balanced them precariously against her stomach, hiding the saucy bears from view.

He smiled as if he'd just licked a dish of cream. 'Lost for words, Randall?'

'Just staggered at your gall,' she said warily.

His big shoulders came to rest against the door-jamb and he reached out to one of the bags to tuck down her favourite pair of satin briefs. 'Wicked extravagance,' he observed.

'They were a present,' she answered shortly. From Ana. 'If you've got anything to say, get on with it. I'm busy.'

'I thought we'd have a chat,' he said and smiled disarmingly. 'I'm sure there's a lot we could say to one another.'

'I doubt it,' she said tersely, her nerves ragged. If he knew about Tom, she thought, she'd rather he said, instead of tormenting her with innuendo. Randall turned on a cool, social smile. 'I really am too busy,' she said lightly. 'Lots of fun things to do. Oven needs cleaning. Bins need emptying. That sort of thing.'

Turning her back, she attempted to get the key out again but her fingers wouldn't reach. His hand slipped into her pocket, his over-sized fist filling the pocket space and pressing intimately through the thin cotton to her curving hip.

'This what you're looking for?' he asked, taking an

unnecessarily long time to withdraw his hand. 'Shall I?'
He waved the key at her.

'Thanks.' She felt the brush of linen against the warm
skin of her naked back and arched away. His pleasantness
worried her. He was after something and she hoped it
wasn't what she imagined.

'There you go.' Julio pushed open the door for her.

'Smashing. Bye.' Thankfully she hastened through.
Hampered by the teetering bags, she was finding it difficult to close the door and kept pushing at it ineffectually.

'My foot's in it,' he explained for her enlightenment.

Her lashes fluttered up in annoyance to find Julio's vel-
vet-black eyes smiling down at her. 'Are you learning to
be a brush salesman or something?' she asked cuttingly.

'We're going to talk,' he said in a reasonable tone that
had razor edges. 'Maybe I'll break the door down, maybe
I'll smash the window. If necessary, I'll drive a bulldozer
straight through the wall, but talk we will. I think you'll
find that the open-door method would save a considerable
amount on the repair bills. I'm out for vengeance,
Randall.'

She felt sick to the stomach. He'd found out. 'Vengeance?' she repeated, her tongue so thick that she spoke
with maddening slowness, even though every nerve was
painfully alert. Revenge: quick, hot, brutal, she thought,
the muscles in her stomach clenching. Not Tom, she
pleaded silently. Please don't let him know about Tom. 'I
can't imagine why.'

Randall sucked in a long breath to calm herself and
played for time by slowly looking him up and down. He
wore the finest cream linen that money could buy. A
cream straw hat on his head. Raw silk shirt, shot cuffs,
gold links and matching tie. Toning soft kid shoes, designer sunglasses tucked in his breast pocket with a cerise
handkerchief.

'Try a little harder,' he said, softly sinister.

He looked smart. Devastating, even. But somehow,

quite deadly. His expression was glacial. The dark eyes would have frozen whisky. And from every pore in his body billowed a hostility so tangible that she felt her skin crawl.

She knew enough of Andalucíans to be aware of the never-forgotten bitterness of old resentments, the long and ruthless pursuit of revenge that followed an insult or a wrong-doing. Shakily she drew in her breath because there didn't seem to be any left in her lungs.

'Oh, dear! It's because I called you a coward, isn't it?' she suggested huskily.

'A minor insult,' he dismissed. 'You're in serious trouble, Randall. Search your memory. Isn't there... something?'

There was an accusing glint of certainty in his malevolent eyes and a void opened up beneath her as she realised she had to accept the inevitable. Above the piled-high bags, her face went ashen, her mouth seemingly filled with clinker.

'Oh, God! How—how did you find out I...?' Her voice became a croak then faded to nothing as his eyes raked her with heartfelt disgust.

'Let me in, you deceitful little bitch, and I'll tell you,' he said softly under his breath as if he didn't trust himself to speak any louder.

He knew. And her lovely cottage was no longer a refuge. More like a trap. 'No. No!' she whispered, feeling sick with trepidation. She could cope with anything but this. Fire, flood, riot, mayhem...anything. So it had come to a tug-of-war, with her son in the middle. And Tom would be destroyed. A shudder ripped through her, the shreds of her self-control vanishing with horror that her ultimate fears had become reality. 'You know, you really do *know*!' she moaned.

'Yes.'

The bags fell to the ground. Julio caught her before she joined them, his arms strong and all-embracing. Her eyes

had closed and somewhere in the distance she could hear
his voice. In her crazy, topsy-turvy world where she'd
retreated, it seemed that he was crooning her name, over
and over again, as he used to when they were young and
deeply in love.

'Julio,' she whispered unhappily in response. 'Julio,
Julio...'

Warmth enclosed an eyelid and then the other like the
softness of a mouth. It made her want to keep her eyes
shut forever. Gentle hands surrounded her face and soft
feathering breath whispered down her cheek, paused fluttering on her gently parted lips and swept on to the pulse
in her throat. Which leapt into shivering life from a moist
caress that forced a low moan from deep inside her body.

'Hell,' came a husky growl. 'Randall!'

Cross that her misty dream was fading, she mumbled a
sulky 'What?'

'Damn you, you little witch!'

Half drunk with a languid indolence, she took her time
opening her eyes, slowly focusing on the heart-stopping
mouth close to hers, its softened lush extravagance temptingly slicked by the tip of a tongue.

'Oh...' she sighed, her lashes fluttering down again.
She was still in the dream.

'I think you'd better sit down.'

It was then that make-believe ended and the real
world—cruel, threatening—exploded into her head with a
force that made her gasp. Her eyes bolted wide open and
she looked around wildly. 'Where—?'

'Santini's cottage. Your cottage, I suppose,' he growled
savagely.

Randall wouldn't look at Julio. She knew with a sickening embarrassment who had featured in her dream,
knew who'd kissed her, taking advantage of her lapse of
consciousness. Stark and huge, her eyes scanned the room
but she didn't take much in. She had a brief impression
of a cool tiled floor, white-painted walls and cheerful yel-

low curtains. And she was sitting in a deep settee, her skirt rumpled...

'Oh!' she croaked and dragged it down over her knees. 'What have you...? How long was I...?' She felt her throat constrict as she turned horrified eyes on the frosty-looking Julio.

'Not long enough for me to rape you,' he said icily, reading her mind with numbing accuracy. 'Though I can't say the thought didn't give me considerable pleasure. Kitchen in there?'

'I don't—' He'd gone. There were background noises of opening cupboards. Randall struggled to compose herself. Julio was plainly furious. He'd come to find out why she'd never told him he had a son by her. And then... what? 'Urrgh...!' she moaned, nausea preventing her from thinking about anything else.

A hand clasped her knee and another clamped on her neck. She fought it, gagging on a choked cry as her neck was forced downwards. 'Keep your head down there if you feel sick,' said Julio sharply. 'Wait a minute. I'll get a cold towel. Where do you keep everything? The place is bare. Don't you spend *any* time in here?' he growled irascibly.

Her hand limply pointed in the vague direction of the bags and he rummaged through her linen. Somehow she managed to regulate her breathing, trying desperately to hold back the nausea because she knew it was imperative that she stayed rational and calm .

'It's cold. Brace yourself,' came Julio's gruff voice.

'Thanks,' she muttered, and shivered as the icy water ran down her naked back. Then she felt satin sliding on her skin and identified it as the lining of Julio's jacket, still warm from his body. And his hand was taking hers, holding the wrist, seeking the pulse. 'I'm OK,' she mumbled, trying to sit up.

'Take it easy. You've had a shock.'

With surprising gentleness, he eased her back and removed the cold cloth, tucking his jacket around her as if she were a child. While he ministered to her, she stared at his lowered lashes, recognising the fact that Tom's would lie in thick black crescents on his cheeks one day.

Dear heaven! she agonised. They were so alike... Could she deny everything? Presumably Julio had seen her with Tom somewhere, somehow. Her mind flew to all kinds of explanations. She could say she'd been baby-sitting. Perhaps pretend Tom was Ana's child... The thought made her wince and drove her into a frenzy of despair. He was *hers.*

'Julio—' she began in a harsh, unrecognisable voice.

'Wait. Talk in a minute. I'm in no rush. I've put the kettle on. I could only find a jar of coffee. It won't be a moment.'

'Let's get it over with,' she said, trembling.

'At least you have some conscience,' he growled. The seat depressed as he sat heavily beside her. When she slanted her eyes at him apprehensively, she saw a nerve quivering at the side of his mouth. He frowned and brought it under control. 'Why, Randall? Why do something like this?' he asked angrily. 'I couldn't believe it at first, despite the overwhelming evidence. But talking to you, discovering the abysmal level of your morals and seeing you here has confirmed all my suspicions—'

'Did you follow me home?' she broke in shakily, not following everything he'd said.

'Home?' He looked puzzled. 'Isn't this your home?'

'Just about. I'm moving in today,' she mumbled.

'That explains the lack of supplies.' Julio frowned and looked at his watch. 'Perhaps we'd better get this unpleasant business settled quickly. I assume the removal men are coming soon.'

She gave a wry, sad smile. 'I don't have anything else. My things are in those bags.'

For a while there was silence. He was looking at them in disbelief. Slowly he went over and checked one of them, unable, it seemed, to accept what she'd said. Randall watched in mute humiliation as he pulled out her pitifully few clothes, some cherished pictures of her father and a collection of small ornaments she and Tom had chosen because he liked frogs and horses. Even Julio looked embarrassed when he turned back again without touching the other bags and walked without a word into the kitchen.

She leaned back and closed her eyes. Having virtually nothing to her name would be damning evidence, she thought unhappily. Julio would say that she wasn't able to care adequately for her son. But Tom was well-fed and clean, she took his education seriously and he had love in abundance. Oceans of it. *Was that enough?* Her pulses bucked and pounded erratically.

'Coffee.' Two mugs appeared on the table. Sitting down again, he studied her silently for several moments, while her heart thudded against her rib-cage and she waited for him to speak till she could stand his scrutiny no more.

'What are you going to do?' she asked dully.

'I'm not sure. I'd like a bit of information about you. Some background.'

She nodded and wet her dry lips. 'Of course.'

'What happened when I left Broadfield?'

In surprise, she turned to stare at him. She was slowly dying inside and he wanted a biography! 'Do you mean the facts or my emotional reaction?' she asked coldly.

'You stayed on at the school?' he asked, unmoved, giving her a lead.

Randall drew in a deep breath. She couldn't bring herself to say that the Head and Steve had helped her financially when Tom had been born. Pride made the words stick in her throat so she decided to skip the nightmare he'd left her in.

She fortified her nerves with a sip of the strong coffee. She couldn't put this off. Naturally he'd want to know how she and Tom had been living up to now. 'I stayed till the Head died,' she said in a low voice. 'That must have been—oh—a year after. Then I had to leave.'

'Why?' he asked with a frown.

Randall heaved a huge sigh. Tom had been tiny, but she'd been turned out of the place where she'd lived all her life, where her darling father had devoted so much of his time and care to cherishing the gardens—and her. All her memories had been cruelly obliterated.

'The headmaster's sons inherited the school,' she said huskily. 'They had no interest in it and sold it to a building firm who razed it to the ground.' He made no comment when she looked sideways at him to see his reaction. It was as if he already knew that Broadfield had vanished. 'All the contents of Dad's tied cottage belonged to the school,' she said miserably. 'I wasn't allowed any keepsakes. Father had never bothered about possessions—the gardens were his passion. I didn't even walk away with a single plant.'

Julio's profile was rock-hard. 'You found work?' he asked curtly.

'Not for two years,' she mumbled, ashamed. No one had wanted to take on a single parent with a small child in tow. Stoically she fought back the self-pity. He wouldn't care how hard the situation had been for her and she dared not make it sound too bad or he'd condemn her for bringing Tom up in conditions of hardship.

'How did you cope?' he asked, far more interested, it seemed, in the crease of his trousers than her plight.

'I don't know!' she yelled, suddenly angry. His eyes snapped up to hers and wishful thinking made her see a flicker of compassion there before she realised it must be a trick of the light. 'I don't know,' she repeated sullenly. 'You do what you have to in circumstances like that.'

'Oh. Yes.' His scornful mouth told her what he imagined *that* to be. 'What made you come here?'

The sadness partially dispelled and her mouth tipped in

a wavering smile. 'Steve. Remember my tutor at evening classes? He always took an interest in me.'

'I remember,' frowned Julio. 'He had the nerve to tell me not to keep hanging around waiting for you to finish classes and to let you get on with your studying.'

'He was only thinking of my welfare,' she explained, recalling how jealous Julio had been of the older man.

'He wanted to break us up—'

'He could have saved his breath, couldn't he?' she said sharply.

'So he moved in,' Julio muttered. 'All that flattery about you being a gifted landscape designer—'

'He meant that!' she said heatedly. 'He knew I could never pass the exams, but he put his faith in me. And put his money where his mouth was, as proof of that trust in my ability.' Her voice grew warm and affectionate as she idly traced her finger around the rim of her mug. 'When he took early retirement, he bought a business in Torremolinos and put me in as manager.'

'Clever move,' said Julio, as coldly condemning as if he were still jealous. 'And you showed your gratitude.'

'Good grief, Julio! I'm not a tramp,' she flared. 'Steve's been a second father to me. He helped me when I was in trouble—which is a darn sight more than you did!' Julio's mouth tightened and she wanted to hurt him, to make him suffer a fraction of what she'd gone through. 'Steve has been loyal to me, acted like a man of honour, two qualities you are in desperate need of!' There. He'd flinched. And it had done her no good at all. She felt depression settle on her and resented him for causing it.

'I don't believe you,' Julio told her flatly.

'I defy you to pin any charge of immorality on me, to find any evidence of my misbehaviour!' she snapped.

'Oh, I will,' he drawled, leaning back, his eyes glittering.

'No. You won't,' she insisted, feeling worried. That was obviously his intention. Slap an immorality order on her, then remove his child. 'Steve has asked for nothing more than friendship,' she snapped. 'Ask anyone who knows us. Some men can be like that, Julio. You'll never understand because—by your own admission—all you think about when you see a woman is what she'd be like stripped naked in your arms and swooning over you.'

'The question was relevant,' he said, unmoved. 'Try to remain rational. Emotion will only cloud the issue. This is something we must sort out between us.'

Rational! When she wanted to howl with rage and violent despair? 'You mean it was relevant in assessing my character? I suppose it was. But are your morals squeaky-clean? Are you reliable? I don't think so. You're the kind of man who walks away from his responsibilities. You let me down, Julio. Badly.' She couldn't say any more. If she voiced any of her heartbreak at this moment, he'd get more emotion than he'd bargained for.

'I'm not under the spotlight. You are,' he snapped. 'Why has this garden business done so badly? Despite difficult times, Marbella is a quality resort. Puerto Banús is awash with money, Torremolinos is full of ex-pats and Málaga groans under the weight of foreign investment. How could you fail? Incompetent management?'

'Thank you for your confidence in me,' she said bitterly. 'No. It's the way things are run out here. There's a group of designers and contractors who are fashionable and that doesn't include me. It's almost impossible to break into the magic circle and get taken up by the big developers, the wealthy owners or the businessmen. I do a lot of the small, less lucrative work. The stuff no one else wants. It's a living. Poor but honest, that's me, and there's nothing unworthy in that. You watched the old films with me, remember?'

Julio looked across at her possessions. 'And that's all you have in the world?' he scowled.

She bit her lip and cast her eyes down, refusing to answer. There was a long pause. Randall's heart and pulses were combining to fill her head with their rapid beating. He'd tell her now, she thought miserably, what he could have provided for his son. And he'd convince her that she'd been wrong to manage alone.

'Is it, Randall?' he persisted harshly.

'I got rid of a lot of stuff when I knew I had this job and was coming here,' she said in all honesty. She gave him a bold stare. 'I'm going to hit the shops next week.'

His steady eyes were quite unblinking. 'That's what you think. Describe where you lived before you moved here,' he ordered.

'You won't be satisfied until you've ground my nose into the dirt, will you?' she muttered. Her pained eyes met his and she felt like dying of shame.

'I'm trying to understand your motives,' he answered, a strange shimmer in his eyes. But his mouth was clamped back tightly as if he were angry with her.

'I suppose you'd find out,' she said listlessly. There was a long pause while she plucked up courage to lay bare the facts of her life-style. Julio drew in an impatient breath and hastily she began to speak. 'I've been living in a rusty caravan in a working yard.' Her head lifted, the humiliation staining her pale cheeks in two bright crimson spots.

'God!' he growled. 'Go on.'

She bit her lip. He must hate the thought of a Quadra in such awful surroundings. More facts to condemn her. Randall fiercely quelled a sob. Tears wouldn't help. 'It's...pretty ugly,' she muttered. 'Packed with junk and garden equipment. Paving slabs. A dump truck, a tipper lorry, compost bags and a selection of plants awaiting delivery. I'm not proud of where I live,' she said, her voice disintegrating along with all her pride. 'But it was a home. People make a home, Julio,' she finished hoarsely. 'People and love and laughter.'

He'd gone to stand by the window and had thrust his hands deep into his trouser pockets, his back straining beneath the fine material of his shirt. It seemed like minutes before he responded, though she supposed it was only a short while. But in that time she'd interpreted the lines of his back and shoulders and had seen how angry he was. Things were beginning to look hopeless for her chances.

'You always needed freedom,' he said quietly. 'Trees, flowers, wildlife…' The broad shoulders lifted and fell again. 'No wonder you took the easy way out,' he muttered.

'Easy!' she cried, with a bitterly ironic laugh. 'You think what I'm doing is easy?'

He spun around on his heel, his eyes blazing black fire. 'Tell me you hate it!' he rasped vehemently.

'No! I don't, I love it, but it isn't easy!' she said crossly. 'Don't denigrate what I do!' He gave a snort and she tossed her head in annoyance. 'You saw the load I was delivering the other day. I'd shovelled that on to the truck first thing in the morning myself and when I delivered it I had to make sure it was in a nice neat pile!' she raged. 'I'm not complaining because I'm completely happy with what I do but I'm not having anyone say it's easy—'

Julio shook his head at her. 'We were at cross purposes. But in any case, I think we've wandered off the subject. All right. So now I have the picture. The question is, will you cause trouble, or will you give him up without any arguments?'

Randall felt the breath leave her body. The nightmare she'd dreaded had begun.

CHAPTER FOUR

IN A rush of adrenalin-powered fury, Randall catapulted out of the seat, driven by the overwhelming instinct to fight for her child. 'Give him up? Are you crazy? Of course I won't!' she yelled.

His teeth bared in a flash of white. Not a smile. An angry grimace. 'Silly question. All right. How about in return for a lump sum?'

Her eyes grew enormous at the suggestion. 'Do—do you think I'd give him up for money?' she spluttered. 'My God, Julio! He means everything to me!'

'Oh, does he.' It was a menacingly soft statement, not a question, as if he found her claim a revelation. She saw that the muscles in Julio's face had become so taut with strain that the bones stood out starkly. 'I'll force you to give in, one way or another,' he said quietly. 'I'll use everything in my power to make sure of that.'

'You bastard!' she whispered. 'You'd take me from him—!'

'I have no choice. My loyalties are to the Quadra.'

Randall bit her lip, afraid she'd be defeated in the end. Who could fight the might of Andalucían ancestors? 'I'll make a concession on my own terms. If you agree to certain rights I wish to preserve, then—then you can...' She couldn't say it, her misty blue eyes blinking at him in utter misery, her lashes wet with tears.

'I can *what*?' he growled remorselessly.

She forced herself to speak. 'Sh-share,' she croaked.

'*Whaaaat*?' Julio grabbed the side of a walnut bookcase as though to steady himself, a look of disgust and horror sweeping over his face. 'You little tramp!' He swore in

65

Spanish, the expletives spilling out in a long stream of uncontrollable fury and mercifully Randall didn't understand most of them. 'Me, share? I *own*,' he snarled through his teeth. 'I don't share! I know you're unconventional, but this…! God help me, Randall, if you're willing to whore for the whole of the Quadra family, I think you ought to know that I would expect sole rights! Three in a bed is *not* an activity I'm eager to try.'

For a moment she didn't understand and then she picked up the innuendo and began to tremble with rage. 'Three in a bed? What the devil are you implying?' she demanded.

'Damn you!' he said irritably. 'Don't start denying it now. You were perfectly ready to admit your involvement with him a short while ago. To my knowledge,' he said, his voice dripping with sarcasm, 'we've been discussing the situation for some time.'

Randall passed a shaking hand over her hot forehead. 'I think there's been a misunderstanding—'

'No,' he snapped. 'Nothing of the kind! You were nervous from the moment we met! Obviously you were afraid I'd find out what you were doing—'

'Well, I—'

'There were those coy remarks you made about knowing a grandee, about bewitching him, about your financial expectations. And there's the fact that you're tucked up in the cottage, nice and handy,' he said scathingly. 'I tried to warn you to steer clear of Santini—'

'Santini?' she repeated stupidly, wondering what this had to do with Tom.

'Of course! Who else are you involved with?' he asked in exasperation. 'You were plainly determined not to take any notice of my warning. You know I'm here to get you out of Santini's hair.'

'I've got no idea what you're talking about!' she cried in total confusion. 'Why should you be concerned with anything I do for Don Carlos?'

Julio's eyes narrowed. 'You do know he's my cousin—and that he's married to my sister, don't you?' he asked slowly.

'Oh! No,' she said weakly. That meant an end to her job. Don Carlos wouldn't employ her. He'd side with Julio. He loved children, asking all about Tom when she said she had a child. And he'd never forgive her for what she'd done either. Her eyes closed in despair. She'd definitely lose her job as well as Tom. She groaned. 'But... how did you find out about me?'

'My sister telephoned me shortly before she left to go on a singing tour. She said that Carlos was having an affair and described the woman she saw him with. That description fits you like a hand fits a glove.' Randall was confused again. 'My sister's honour is my responsibility,' Julio continued relentlessly. 'I've been staying with friends and keeping an eye on Carlos while she's away. Now I know who his mistress is, I intend to end your relationship with him—one way or another.'

Relationship? He thought... Her mind whirled, going back over their recent conversation. It slowly dawned on her that Julio's anger might be nothing to do with Tom after all!

'I said "share" and you thought—' She gulped. Three in a bed! 'Good grief!' she blazed. 'Let me get this clear. You think I'm your cousin's mistress—and that's why you're here? Why pick on me? I'm not the only blonde around, you know!'

'You're the only one who fits the description and has been settled in a cottage on Quadra land,' growled Julio.

'And that's...all? The only reason you're here?' she asked in blank-faced astonishment.

'All? *All*? Why else would I want to come here to see you?' he glared. 'Did you imagine I'd come to heat up a woman who's yesterday's dinner?'

The insult never touched her. She sat down in a heap and began to laugh. The clouds had vanished from her horizons, the expected storm had come to nothing. Relief, hope and a wonderful sense of deliverance from despair washed through her in waves, obliterating all her fear and her misery. Emotionally uncontrolled, her laughter grew shriller and wilder, until she felt a stinging blow on the side of her face. 'Ohhh!' she gasped in shock.

'I'm sorry.' Stony-faced, Julio knelt in front of her, his hand gently massaging her tingling cheek. 'You seemed hysterical. Did I hurt you?'

'No—yes—it doesn't matter,' she said, her eyes sparkling with unconcealed joy. Her secret was safe. A great burst of energy tempted her to grab him and dance around the room. 'Oh, you're priceless!' she laughed, shaking her head. 'Santini's lover! That's the most *ridiculous* thing I've ever heard!'

Her shoulder was gripped by a vice-like hand. 'You can't laugh it off,' he growled. 'I admire your spirit. I applaud your ability to keep cheerful. But I'm not fooling, Randall. You'll give him up. Today.'

'Oh, listen to me! You've got it all wrong,' she said, unable to hold back a silly grin of relief. Tom was safe! Who cared about anything else? 'Julio,' she gurgled. 'You're way off beam! I don't know who this woman can be, but it certainly isn't me. Don Carlos seems too decent a man to have a casual affair—'

'God, are you still naïve?' scorned Julio.

She bristled. 'Whatever the case, he isn't my lover and that's the gospel truth.'

'Don't be difficult!' complained Julio irritably. 'This can be done with dignity, or it can be messy. It's your choice—'

'Messy?' Where had she heard that before recently? The penny dropped. 'You were planning this all along! I was the woman you intended to flay alive!' she exclaimed.

'And still might,' he threatened. 'OK. Let's deal. I know what your expectations were. You thought you were going to get filthy rich from this relationship. I suppose you don't want to lose any advantages you would gain by living here—'

'You're darn right I don't!' she cried indignantly.

'Then I'll bargain with you,' he said. 'I appreciate it probably suits your twisted sense of justice to fleece my cousin. I can make things easier for you, save you the trouble of getting into bed with him. If your ambitions run to having a new wardrobe and a better lifestyle, then I'm prepared to provide that. On the condition you leave Santini and swear never to communicate with him again.'

Randall slid from beneath the insistent pressure of Julio's hand and rose in a smooth, fluid movement, all her self-assurance restored. 'You're determined to see me as a modern Jezebel, aren't you?' she said coolly, walking to her bags and searching for some biscuits. 'And you couldn't be more wrong. I'm working for your cousin— I had an interview the other day—'

'For two hours.' He unwound his legs and strolled over to her, his glittering eyes holding hers with an icy anger. 'I was in the summerhouse, checking on who came and who went. I saw you arrive, I saw you in the bedroom, you little tramp, and I waited to see how long you'd stay.'

'You can be pretty determined when you want something,' she said quietly. 'But it wasn't like that. We went up to the bedroom so that your cousin could show me where the cottage was and how I could reach it from the back gate.'

'Of course!' he murmured sardonically. 'The explanation's simple. Why didn't I think of that?'

'Because you have a nasty suspicious mind,' she countered sweetly. 'And it was a long interview, but we had tea and chatted,' she added serenely, convinced he'd see how silly it all was in a moment, if she persevered. Contentedly she munched the biscuit, her eyes smiling at him with supreme confidence. Tom was safe. All that mattered.

'Stupid of me not to realise. One often has tea and a

friendly chat with one's prospective gardener. Good God, Randall!' he exploded. 'In this country? A man doesn't invite a woman in and talk to her for two hours without an ulterior motive! Do you really think you can get away with this rubbish? What in the name of sanity can you have been talking about, all that time?'

Mainly my son, she thought fondly. Santini had obviously longed for children of his own. 'My background,' she said truthfully. 'What I'd been doing, which contractors I worked for, my ambitions. Things like that.'

'He handed you a front door key—'

'To the cottage.' She smiled at his angry face and said gently, 'Gardener's perks. Admit it—your evidence is very flimsy, Julio.'

'I don't think so. Anyone seeing you two saying goodbye on the doorstep would assume you were intimate,' he said grimly. 'In Andalucía, it simply isn't done for a married man to touch a woman with such familiarity.'

Randall looked discomfited. Santini's arm had been around her shoulders and, knowing the local moral codes, that had bothered her a little. But she'd put that down to his obvious concern for Tom and herself living in the awful yard, the emotional response of a childless man who loved children and was contemplating the pleasure of hearing the sound of a child's laughter every day.

'If you know Don Carlos well,' she said quietly, 'then you'll be aware that he has a heart of gold. He's a very caring, warm and passionate man, Julio.' Her eyes glinted dangerously at his sardonic snort.

'He adequately displayed this care, warmth and passion during your interview, I imagine,' mused Julio nastily. 'It occurs to me that something more than tea must have caused your...effervescence.'

'You're so right,' she said fervently. 'Apart from offering me a marvellous job and a decent home, your cousin was telling me that he was perfectly prepared to recommend me to his friends if he liked the way I revamped the pool area. Don't spoil this,' she pleaded. 'It's important to me,' she explained with increasing passion. 'Your cousin's patronage could open all the doors that have been closed up to now. It means I won't be refused work any more because I'm a woman and an outsider. Surely you can understand why I was absolutely bowled over by his kindness?'

Julio's eyes were veiled. 'Oh, yes. It's the way he works. Slow seduction is an Andalucían speciality. Crafty bastard!' he muttered. 'OK. I've had enough of this. I want you out of here and off this land. I'm trying to be reasonable and I'll see you have money if it'll keep you quiet. That's more than generous under the circumstances. But I insist you stay away from my cousin.'

'Insist all you like. I won't be falsely accused and bullied by you,' she answered flatly. 'You're not going to spoil my future. Just try accusing me of adultery in public, and I'll prove I'm innocent and make you look an absolute fool. That's all I have to say on the subject. Would you close the door when you leave?'

'I'm surprised you dare to defy me,' he said softly. 'You'll regret doing so. I'm going to collect my luggage from where I've been staying. And then I'm letting Santini know that I've arrived in Spain and I'm after his hide. I'll force him to sack you within the hour.'

'You wouldn't!' she gasped in dismay.

'Santini does what I tell him. If I say "jump", he jumps. Athletic of him, isn't it? Though I suppose,' he mused unpleasantly, 'you know that already.'

'You foul, vengeful—!'

'Do you admit your affair or not?' he snapped.

'*No*!'

His thumb and forefinger gripped her chin and pushed it up till she was forced to look into his contemptuous dark eyes. Her palms braced the distance between them, shaping to the curve of his chest. There was a powerful assault on her senses as they picked up the slight rough slub weave in the linen, the silkiness of the shirt and the hot warmth of the man beneath. Her nostrils quivered once again at the well-remembered fragrances that hung around him, elusive, subtle and exotic.

'Such a pity,' he said softly. 'I'm sorry if poverty has forced you to prostitute yourself. I'm prepared to keep you out of trouble—'

'Keep your filthy money!' she said proudly. 'Leave me alone. Take the next flight home!' She felt his hands on her back where the halter-neck top left her skin bare and she gritted her teeth at the slow, gentle movement. Like a stupid doll, she stood there, quivering from the electric storm raging between them. It wasn't happening to her, she thought miserably, feeling control slipping away.

'I'll make you see sense if I have to tie you up in a sack and dump you in the gorge to do so,' he muttered.

The slide of his fingers was maddening and she suffered it with difficulty. Yet if she arched away from his fingers, she knew she'd be virtually pressing her breasts against the heated wall of his chest. His hand drifted to the bow that tied her top. 'Leave it!' she snapped.

'I'm not sure I can.'

His voice was a whisper and she abandoned her cold, blind stare at the rich sheen of his throat to gauge his intentions. What she saw in his expression caused a minor eruption inside her. The blatant sexual appraisal seemed to turn her into an electrically charged field and she could sense an unstoppable force pulling them towards each other. 'No,' she whispered.

'I—want—you,' he said very, very slowly. 'God, how…I…want…you.'

Her eyes dilated as his mouth approached hers. A faint whimper came from her throat and he'd roughly hauled her against his body, her curves softening against his hard flesh and bone. The hungry depths of his eyes held her as surely as if they'd been welded together but she tried, against all her headstrong instincts, she tried. 'Don't,' she moaned.

'Can't you imagine how satisfying it will be?' he murmured in a gently persuasive voice. 'We're not young lovers, meeting passion for the first time. We'd be more aware. Take more enjoyment from each other. Give more.'

His hand swept beneath her hair, lifting it from her neck, his fingers threading through the golden strands. And she lifted her face in an involuntary sigh of pleasure as his fingertips worked up her scalp in small, rhythmic movements.

'Julio,' she mumbled in a feeble protest. And then, 'Julio,' which was more of a husky sigh, a call of need from deep within her subconscious.

'We could pretend we're by the river,' he said, his voice slurring with desire. Her shoulders were raided by small kisses, brief, hot... not enough, not enough! she wanted to shout. And then her throat felt the softness of his mouth and she could smell the clean warmth of his hair as her head tipped back, far back, to accommodate him.

'The river...?'

'Where,' he reminded her, taking the lobe of her ear in his mouth, 'we made love in the dead of night.'

'I don't remember,' she lied stubbornly.

He paused in his tasting of her soft flesh as her fingers dug into his shoulders hard. It had been wonderful. He'd promised to touch every inch of her body with his mouth. With love. And his mouth, now offering her only desire, began to whisper across the sensitised satin of her skin towards her waiting lips.

'You're more beautiful now,' he crooned. 'Irresistible... Perfect, incredibly sexy...'

Randall swayed in his arms as she waited in helpless anticipation for his kiss. In her mind she could feel his slowly exploring mouth now, the sheer joy of it, and put her fingers to her lips as a sudden spasm of hunger hit her like a punch in the stomach.

'Memories stir you, do they?' he said lazily, his lashes fluttering on his high Spanish cheekbones.

'No!' she whispered. 'Go to hell!' she rasped out in desperation.

He laughed harshly and released her, his eyes as fathomless as night. 'If you only knew,' he husked. 'Relax,' he mocked, as Randall continued to watch him like a wary fawn. 'I'll investigate one or two of those deliciously hidden cute juggling bears another time.'

'There won't be another time!' she muttered viciously. 'Go and see Don Carlos! He'll defend me! And you'll feel *stupid*!'

The dark brows quivered with the flinch that narrowed his eyes. 'You're very confident,' he said softly. 'You must have quite a hold on Carlos. Maybe you're more dangerous than I imagined.'

'I don't have any hold on him. I'm innocent.'

He strode purposefully to the door then turned to face her, his eyes blisteringly angry. 'Lying little tramp!' he grated. 'You, innocent? You were paralysed with horror that I'd found out your secret. You even told me you wouldn't give him up. Remember? Get your story straight, Randall,' he said in contempt.

She blinked and blushed guiltily. Julio waited for a fraction of a second in case she explained, but she stared at him in despair, her wits deserting her entirely. 'What are you going to do?' she asked in agitation. 'Don't lose me this job—'

'You're wasting your time,' he drawled. 'Get out while the going's good. When I've seen my friends, I'll face my cousin with his infidelity. After that, I'll break each one of his fingers, joint by joint, and, if I'm still angry, I'll start on his ribs. Then I'll come for you.'

He gave her a mocking smile and strolled out, leaving the door wide open. Suddenly her face went as white as a sheet. His accusations could be laughed off since they could be disproved, but Santini knew that Tom was almost five and in denying their affair—perhaps by trying to placate the vengeful Julio—he might let that fact slip. Julio had been a brilliant mathematician. Working out the date of Tom's conception would hardly be beyond him. Her son's future was still in danger.

She had one slim chance. Santini might listen to her and believe her. She had to beg—not only for his support, but for his silence. *Now*. Julio's friends might only live a short distance away and he could be grilling the unsuspecting Santini within ten minutes or so. She dismissed her worries about Don Carlos's reaction to her odd request. Or her presumption in approaching him so boldly. They were the least of her problems.

'Damn you, Julio!' she muttered. He was forcing her to go to a man who'd treated her decently and out of the blue inform him that he'd been accused of having an affair with her! How did you say something like that?!

She stumbled outside to find that Julio had already disappeared. Gritting her teeth, she took a short cut through the overgrown shrubbery, emerging with scratches on her body and leaves in her hair. Overwhelmed by conflicting emotions, she dashed across the open terrace and burst recklessly into the drawing-room where Carlos Santini's slight figure was lounging.

'What the—!' he exclaimed, almost spilling his tumbler of Pimm's in astonishment.

She came to a halt. This was transgressing. Stepping over the line. Peasants didn't beard noblemen in their lairs. She bit her lip. No time for niceties.

Plunging straight in, she haltingly explained that Julio had accused her of being his mistress. For a moment there was a silence. It would be nice, she thought, scarlet with shame, if a huge hole opened up in the ground beneath her, right at this moment.

'Julio…is *here*?' said Santini slowly. He pushed a hand

through his thinning dark hair, appearing to be digesting that information with some difficulty. 'And...he is accusing *you* of... The devil!' He smiled to himself in wry amusement. 'Fortune smiles on me.' Randall gaped in surprise and he suddenly started. 'I'm so sorry. I appreciate how upset you must be,' he murmured smoothly recovering his composure.

'I can't tell you how embarrassing this is,' she mumbled.

Far from being shocked, Santini seemed very concerned about her and warmly took her trembling hands in his. She stepped back, a little alarmed, but he drew her closer again and she felt it would be rude at that moment to pull away.

'It's not your fault. I'm afraid my wife is very jealous,' he said smoothly. 'It's difficult, being the husband of an opera singer. No doubt she saw me with the English rep I met at a country club, to discuss the new sunbeds for the pool. Or,' he mused as another thought occurred to him, 'there is the possibility that my wife has hit on the only reason that would prise Julio from his home.'

'I see,' she said cautiously, somehow not certain any longer. Perhaps she was naïve.

Santini's thin mouth twitched. 'I'm grateful for the warning. I owe you more than you know. If I have to swear on oath before a priest, I'll convince Julio that you are not my mistress—and make sure you don't lose your job.'

'An oath?' That was enough to convince her of Santini's innocence. 'Oh, thank you!' she cried with heart-felt gratitude and relief. 'I have such a lot to thank you for.'

'I suppose you do,' murmured Santini modestly, his eyes lowered.

'And...about Tom—' she said awkwardly. It seemed that she was asking a lot of her new employer and putting herself in his debt. 'I don't want people to know that I have a child—'

He stroked her hand soothingly but it made her more agitated. 'You don't want potential clients to think you're…cheap. I understand. It would make you rather vulnerable to unscrupulous men,' he said huskily. Randall suddenly went cold. Was she imagining the predatory look in Santini's eyes? 'Julio won't find out,' he continued softly. 'We must talk about this later, tonight, perhaps—'

His breath rasped in harshly. She was being pushed away and following Santini's startled eyes, she saw Julio standing in the open doorway as motionless as a statue.

'How—how long have you been there?' she asked nervously, frantically trying to recall what they'd said about Tom. 'You've been spying on us!' she accused.

'I wonder why,' he drawled, briefly acknowledging his cousin with a curt, cold nod. 'Leave us, Randall,' Julio said, his voice barely above a harsh whisper. Neither she nor Santini seemed capable of moving. 'Go through that door and wait. Or I'll help you through—none too gently.'

'You—you said you were going to your friend's house—' she began jerkily.

'I lied. What better way to see if you'd go running to your lover with the bad news?' said Julio unpleasantly. 'Now get out. I have a few things to discuss that your ears should never hear.'

'Julio!' cried Santini warily. 'I can explain—'

'Wait!' barked Julio. 'Family business is discussed in private! This woman is supposed to be your gardener! Have you no discretion?' He shot a furious look at the stunned Randall. 'Get out of here when I tell you!' he snarled.

He was too angry to be defied; it would only make matters worse. Miserably she walked through the door Julio had indicated and found herself in a cloistered gallery that surrounded a central courtyard where a fountain and lush planting made a cool retreat from the sun. Aching from tension, she sat on the walled edge of the fountain and covered her face with shaking hands.

It was degrading, having someone believe that she was capable of adultery and shadowing her as if she were a common criminal. It pained her that Julio should think so badly of her. All she could do was to put her faith in Santini—and in her innocence. Her fingers trailed idly in the water. The next few minutes could well decide her future.

A silent eternity later, she heard a footfall and lifted her head in apprehension. Julio's face was without expression. 'Well?' she asked breathlessly.

He sat on the edge of the fountain in front of her so that they were almost knee to knee. 'Carlos was very convincing,' he said laconically. 'But then he usually is. However, the description of his mistress was extremely detailed... Hair, weight, colour of eyes, shape of body... My sister said on the telephone that the woman looked...' Pausing thoughtfully, he moistened his lips as though they were dry. 'As if she were about to dance or sing for joy, a woman who was eager to grab life by the throat and enjoy every second to the full.' He gave a small laugh. 'That's exactly the way I remembered you.' His eyes met hers. 'I thought of you at once,' he husked.

'So you were virtually programmed to look for someone like me, even before you'd left Argentina,' she pointed out resentfully.

'Perhaps. In any case, the first woman I saw hanging around the house *was* you.' He scowled at the crystal water. 'I was shocked to think of you being bedded by my cousin.'

'You have no right to feel any emotion about me!' she protested. 'You'd given me up. You yourself had released the ties. I wish you'd go home, Julio,' she said shakily. 'Surely you're missing...'

Randall bit her lip, unable to think of him pining for

Elvira and her sentence was left unfinished. There was pain in her eyes. Her lashes lowered and she saw his hands clenched on his knees; square, practical—a gardener's hands, which she'd once believed would always hold her safe from all the hurt in the world. Sadly, nothing was ever that certain.

'I'll leave when I'm one hundred per cent certain,' he said curtly. 'Missing home or not, duty comes first.'

She heaved a sigh of resignation. 'Of course.' It always had. Dismay engulfed her as the implications of his decision hit her with a sickening impact. As long as he stayed in Spain, she dared not bring Tom to live with her.

Randall stared hopelessly down, her eyes vaguely focused on the ruthlessly sharp pleat in his elegant trousers while she tried to think. Eventually Julio would discover that she wasn't Santini's mistress, but...

Her eyes brightened at the glimmer of an idea. In the meantime maybe Tom could stay with Ana till it was safe! Ana loved children and had five of her own. Tom adored the happy atmosphere in Ana's house and there were always kittens and puppies around.

She cheered up a little. It would be perfectly possible for her to spend all her spare time at Ana's without arousing suspicion. Bravely she quelled her distress at the thought of being parted from her child and tried to be sensible. The only difference, she argued, would be that she and Tom wouldn't sleep in the same house, or have breakfast together. Randall sighed inwardly. She had no alternative, hard though it would be.

The decision made, she rose to her feet. 'Since I'll be working here, I expect I'll see you around, then,' she said politely.

'Behind,' he amended, his eyes mocking. 'I'll be following every move you make. I mean to ensure that my sister's marriage is not threatened,' he said softly.

'Oh.' She quivered at the idea of being stalked by Julio. But she'd evaded him up to now—she could do so again.

Her eyes glinted with rebellion. 'Waste your time if you wish,' she said flatly. 'You're going to be *dreadfully* bored.'

She turned on her heel and walked from the garden but her anger was turning to a grim determination to make Julio regret his decision to follow her. A slow smile curled her lips. In her mind she was plotting trips that would make Julio regret his suspicions. Laughter bubbled from her for the first time in ages. It would be a tiny, but highly satisfying revenge and she was looking forward to it immensely.

Fifteen minutes later, almost excited at the prospect of making the running for a change, she was dashing out of the cottage in a bright yellow dress with a simple shirt collar and a feminine circular skirt. The release from worrying about Tom's security had cheered her immeasurably and she sang-alonga-flamenco as she drove to Ronda, to do some shopping and to ring Ana.

Her eyes lit up with a malicious glee when she noticed the black Lamborghini behind her. 'Julio!' she giggled. His wrap-around sunglasses shone malevolently at her. So she slipped her hand out of the window and waggled her fingers in a cheeky wave. He raised his hand in ironic salute. She felt a sense of being challenged; this would be a battle of wits. And she'd lead him by the nose!

Deliberately hoping to annoy him, she drove in and out of the labyrinth of narrow streets in the old Moorish part of the town, stopping, backing up, turning off at a whim as if sightseeing. Soon she was, enjoying the sleepy ambience of the picturesque whitewashed houses, bright with geraniums that tumbled from bellying iron balconies. By an alabaster spring, she drew her truck to a halt and watched a beautifully dressed young man kneeling by a low, grilled window. Very quietly she slid out of the cab, intending to take a walk. But the couple captivated her attention.

The sleek black car purred up beside her. Julio stuck

his head out of the window and she gave him an insincere smile. 'Isn't it fun playing Follow My Leader?' she said coolly.

Her remark seemed to catch him unawares, because he laughed, his white teeth slashing the darkness of his face. 'Wicked woman,' he chided mockingly. 'Are we stopping long enough for me to turn off my engine?'

'Depends. What's that young man doing?' she asked curiously. 'Praying?'

'For slim ankles, maybe,' he drawled, switching off the catlike purr. 'He's courting.'

'Down there?' she marvelled. A languid arm fluttered through the grille. The young man took it, kissed it passionately and gazed into his sweetheart's eyes. 'How romantic!' she sighed.

'It's an old tradition,' explained Julio softly in the hot silence of the late afternoon. 'There'll be a duenna acting as chaperon in the room behind the girl. But they can talk and touch—within reason—providing the grille remains between them. Sweet pain.' He smiled and slid off his sunglasses, his dark eyes immediately capturing Randall's. 'So close to the illicit thrill of temptation, so agonisingly far from releasing it.'

His voice was low and murmuring with an underlying passion as he savoured the young man's torment. There was no moderation in this country, she thought wryly, feeling the tension in the air. Purity and sex went hand in hand. Stifling restraint fought fiery emotions.

The heat sat heavily on the small square, each window shuttered and silent, forbidding, austere—yet each balcony spilled over with intense-hued geraniums, blowsy begonias, tasselled love-lies-bleeding, papaver, verbena, argyranthemum, passion flower, plumbago... Restraint and exuberance.

The young man plucked a convenient pure white rose— not so convenient, perhaps, because below the perfect bloom the thorns were sharp enough to slash his eager hand. He was rewarded with fluttering eyelashes and a gently attentive dab of the girl's lacy handkerchief.

'It could almost be the courtship of a knight and his lady. Quite medieval,' she said softly, touched by the scene. It told her more about Andalucía than she'd learnt in two years of living in Torremolinos.

'A glimpse of a cheek, a flutter of a woman's lashes was sufficient then to arouse men to a frenzy. Maybe it still does,' murmured Julio pensively.

'A glimpse of a cheek…' She had unwittingly exposed far more when they'd been together in the past—and recently. No wonder he'd been aroused. 'I must have seemed a strange, wild creature to you, when you came to Broadfield,' she said slowly.

He quietly opened his car door and stepped out, leaning against the gleaming coachwork, his eyes slowly admiring every inch of her. She was barely aware of this, too engrossed in the fact that he'd rolled his sleeves up and that she was transfixed by the dauntingly male strength of his forearms. He was bigger, tougher, meaner than before, she mused. More of an unknown entity. She gave a little shiver.

'Astonishing,' he was saying, when she pulled her attention back.

'What is?' she asked guiltily.

'You had an amazing amount of freedom,' he observed. 'Your father didn't even worry if you missed school. And he made no attempt to watch over you, when you grew into a young woman.'

Randall struggled against the soft lure of his mouth, the caressing sound of his voice as it flowed over her like warm satin on a naked body. Compared with the women of his home country, she'd been totally available.

'Father trusted you,' she breathed. The serious depths of his limpid eyes seemed intent on binding her to him—and close to succeeding.

'He was a good man, with no dark thoughts about anyone. But I never trusted myself,' Julio answered huskily, his eyes mesmeric. 'I tried to keep my hands off you. For a long time I resisted. But I felt compelled to look, to touch, to anticipate the pleasure... I wanted to savour everything about you to the full, slowly, spinning it out. The perfume of your hair, the softness of your skin...'

His drowsily spoken words faded away and he was silent, watching the effect they were having on her. So close, she thought. So far. Inside, her body pulsated with a thudding urgency, tantalised, aroused, it seemed, only to be denied satisfaction.

Unwillingly, she felt the same terrible tug of her senses. 'I can see how you were driven beyond control. We were together too much—thrown into each other's company.' She tried a grin but it didn't quite come off. 'I'd got used to wearing my old shorts and sun-tops and never gave them a thought. Looking back, they must have been a bit indecent.'

'I did find your casual attitude about your body increasingly difficult to handle,' he murmured. 'And something of a challenge to my male pride.'

'I honestly didn't know what it was doing to you,' she said huskily, her eyes hypnotised by his infinitely seductive expression. Somehow she managed to smile too. It had been sex, not love, that had churned up their emotions. Ignorant of both, she'd confused the two, and had believed that the overwhelming feelings that had possessed her were due to true love.

'Innocence can cause mayhem,' frowned Julio. He turned to watch the young lovers.

The young man was presenting his girl with a small book—love poems, perhaps?—and Randall's heart warmed. With some difficulty, she tried to turn the conversation. 'It's an entirely different world here from the coast, isn't it?' she said in a conversational tone, dismayed how banal that sounded. 'Almost another country, another time.'

'You're right. This is the real Spain,' he said lovingly. "The old Spain. It still exists, despite the new permissiveness. The Costa is…international in its outlook. Here, we obey the old code of honour.' He slanted his eyes at her. 'Are you horrified by the strict rules of behaviour that those two are forced to observe? I imagine you find it offends all the progress of female emancipation to learn that some of our women are cloistered and protected till their wedding-day.'

'They accept it,' she said softly. 'I'm perfectly aware of the concept of female honour out here. This is your tradition, your standards. That's all that matters. My opinion is irrelevant. They look happy,' she said wistfully. Her expression was tender, her blue eyes soft with envy. 'They're very much in love,' she husked.

'May God keep them so,' muttered Julio fervently.

Her eyes rested thoughtfully on his impassioned face. He wasn't being cynical. He had meant every word. Somewhere in that angry, bitter heart lay a romantic, sensitive man, and she was glad. A mist blurred her vision and Randall realised with astonishment that she was close to tears. How stupid! she thought, amazed at herself. And her sentimentality worried her. Julio was married and apparently determined to hurt her for some inexplicable reason, perhaps driven by deep urges to seduce her again. It was vital that she remember how vulnerable she was and that Julio was totally ruthless. And unassailable.

CHAPTER FIVE

SHE had to be tough like him, as unconcerned and as determined to make things go her way. There was a terrible penalty to pay if she once let Julio get the better of her; Tom's future and her own were inextricably bound up in how well she stood up to Julio's persistent attacks on her reputation and her senses.

'Well, now,' Randall said brightly. 'Are we off in convoy again? I hope you like shopping. If you prefer,' she offered generously, 'I'll tell you where I'm going to save you sliding furtively around the corners of buildings and diving into doorways.'

He laughed, the lines of his face relaxed and friendly. 'I think I blew my undercover status before I even started, don't you? And though the excitement's killing me, I enjoy being surprised. Since you love teasing, carry on. Amuse yourself.'

'I'll do my best,' Randall said solemnly. 'Ready?'

He gave her a wicked grin that was dangerously close to stealing her heart. 'Wherever you go, I go,' he murmured. 'Lead on.'

'It's the most unlikely convoy,' she said drily. 'A battered old truck and a flashy penthouse on wheels.

He laughed again. For a few seconds she gazed at him, bewildered and worried by the alarmingly affectionate feelings she had for the new, elated Julio. They'd only shared a few moments together, gazed at a couple of lovers, chatted cautiously around the subject of morality. But the atmosphere between them had changed and so had he. Julio seemed alive again—vital, brimming with life…and far too dangerous to be allowed out without his wife.

'Get going, Randall,' he said softly, touching her mouth with a speculative, questing finger that took her breath away. 'Before I break a few rules,' he continued, more hoarsely than before, 'and show that young man over there what he's missing.'

'So rules are all right for you to break, but not for your cousin?' she said scathingly.

'I don't get involved. He does.'

Haughtily she climbed into the truck. The engine roared into life, choked, and—by dint of her expert footwork on the pedals—recovered itself. When she drove off she noticed that the lovers had not even paused in their mutual adoration when the truck's noisy coughing had split the peaceful street. The world stopped for lovers, she sighed sentimentally.

Her romantic mood was reinforced when she drove slowly across the spectacular bridge spanning the gorge that split the impregnable town of Ronda in two. Tall, whitewashed houses perched on the precipitous edges, hundreds of feet above the silver-ribboned river below. Young men lounged against the parapet of the bridge, talking and eyeing the erect young women who walked by with their slumbrous eyes fixed firmly ahead, their swaying hips a silent invitation.

Pride and the disapproval of the all-important community held their intense passion in check, she mused, finding it easier now to understand Julio. As a young man, feeling the first stirrings of sexual desire, he must have spent his holidays among women like that: alluring, sensuous, but strictly off limits.

Then he'd returned to the friendly intimacy they'd always enjoyed. She groaned. And how! Pity she'd never known what her role had been in his life. And what now? Was he experiencing the same need to let off sexual steam, now he was surrounded by the beautiful women of Andalucía? Carnally repressed men were potential dynamite, she thought wryly, as she parked in the Plaza de España.

The Lamborghini oozed to a halt beside her truck. Julio uncurled himself from the low, flamboyant car and handed her down, helping her to balance on the rusty steps. 'I'll be right behind you,' he said, his hooded eyes lingering on the swell of her hips, then the cinched waist and her high breasts.

'I'd better walk sedately, then,' she said wryly.

'You can't. Everything swings,' he said lazily.

'Does it?' she asked anxiously, her hands clamped to her hips as though she could hold her body rigid.

'Take note of the reactions,' he drawled.

Walking as demurely as possible, she wandered around, haughtily ignoring the frank stares from the Spanish Africa legionnaires in their tropical green coats and tasselled fezes. But that was to be expected. Every Spanish male took an interest in women and she smiled when Julio scowled at a group of soldiers who'd murmured their appreciation as she emerged from a grocery shop.

'I'll take the bags.' Julio's glare made the soldiers turn hastily away.

'Thank you.' She flashed him a disarming smile and checked her watch. Ana would be home now, after taking the children swimming. Time to phone. Deliberately she let one of the bags slip so that a load of apples tumbled out on to the pavement. 'Whoops!' she cried gaily.

'I'll get them,' he said courteously, as she knew he would.

'You're a doll!' she chirruped. 'Excuse me.'

She ran off, delighted at her cunning. Weaving through the strolling people, she slipped quickly into a tapas bar where she located the telephone and eagerly dialled Ana's number. First she spoke to her friend—who laughed and said one more child would make no difference—and then she spoke to Tom, her face softening with tender love when she heard his voice.

'It'll be a lovely holiday!' she cried, injecting excitement into her voice.

'You won't be sleeping near me,' he objected uncertainly. 'And you won't be there for breakfast.'

She heard the quiver in his voice and had to steel herself to be cheerful. 'Darling,' she said softly, and told him how special her job was and of all the things they'd do once he came to live in the cottage with her. 'Can you be grown up enough to wait a little while?' she coaxed. 'Ana has promised that you can feed the puppies in the morning. I'll see you almost as much as if we were still in the caravan. And think what there is to look forward to!' she cried enthusiastically. 'It'll be like waiting for Christmas. What fun when we're together again!'

Glad that he couldn't see her, she dabbed at her eyes.

'Can we have a puppy one day, when you're rich?' Tom asked hopefully. 'We'd have a garden for it to play in.'

'Oh, I think we might!' she said and smiled at her son's excited cheer.

Julio strolled in, his graceful, indolent walk riveting every woman in the noisy bar. His dark velvet eyes met hers reproachfully, but she knew he'd never hear anything of her conversation from where he stood, because there was such an unholy din. Nevertheless, she turned her back. She wouldn't be surprised if lip-reading was one of his million skills.

'I must go. Bye, darling,' she said wistfully. 'Have a lovely time. Ana's taking you all swimming. I won't see you tonight. Tomorrow if I can. Bye. I love you. I love you, very, very much.' And blew him kisses because he insisted.

Randall replaced the receiver reluctantly, longing to visit him that night to read his bedtime story. Without Tom it would be as though part of her was missing. But she dared not risk it. She'd try to shake Julio off tomorrow, though, and even if he did follow, he'd only see her with friends, playing with their *six* children. There was safety in a crowd.

For a few moments she let the feelings of loss wash over her, gradually finding the steel within herself that would help her to get through the next few days.

In fact, she thought, she'd been rather clever to outwit Julio. If she worked non-stop, the time would go quickly, and she could get the cottage fixed up—perhaps even buy that puppy. Her head lifted. It felt as if a weight had lifted from her shoulders. Rather pleased with her handling of the situation, she made her way between the tables and the bar, smiling smugly at Julio as she passed by.

'Couldn't resist giving you the slip,' she murmured. 'I felt trapped with you dogging my heels. Had to find a few moments to myself.'

'The phone call?' he queried softly.

She smiled. 'Rang my girlfriend. Told her I had a sinister-looking man following me.' Her eyes fluttered in a mock flirt with his. She shouldn't have done that. You fool, she told herself, seeing the instant smouldering response.

'You're quite a tease,' he murmured. 'Have a drink with me.' His hand detained her. 'And some tapas.'

She was about to refuse but realised she hadn't eaten for some time. Sitting in a bar was safe enough. 'I don't suppose there's any harm in letting you buy me a meal,' she said generously. 'All right. I'll have fresh orange, prawns, goat's cheese and…' Her eyes alighted on the ready-prepared dish of assorted tiny fish. '*Fritura mixta*, please. And ham. And—'

'Over-the-top again, Randall! I'd forgotten how thoroughly you ate!' he said, amused, as the barman lined everything up for her.

She gave her undivided attention to the sizzling goat's cheese. 'This is gorgeous!' she sighed enthusiastically. Avoiding his warm eyes, she glanced around the bar, smiling at the way everyone seemed compelled to talk at the tops of their voices. 'Such a volatile lot, the Spanish,' she observed. 'I love them.' Her eyes sparkled and she gazed contentedly at everyone packed around her, receiving a few calls of '*Salud!*' and raised glasses in acknowledgement of her warm smile.

'You really are happy, aren't you?' Julio mused.

'I have a lot to be happy about,' she replied, her voice gentle as she thought of Tom and the chance to give him the kind of future he deserved.

His hand touched her hair in a contemplative gesture. 'That's what I've always liked about you. I'm surprised some man hasn't snapped you up to bring joy into his life. And other delights,' he said with a crooked grin.

Trying to appear casual—even if all her pulses were hammering with the light touch of his fingers just behind her ear—she gave a shrug and popped a prawn into her mouth to take her mind off his sensual caress. 'Dear old-fashioned thing,' she teased. 'I'm not on this earth to be snapped up and bring joy into a man's life. I'm here to be happy. I can do that without a husband, thanks.'

'So you make do with…relationships?' he suggested, his eyes veiled. 'Like the man who means everything to you? One lover or two?' Her mouth twitched. 'Three?'

'Try seven,' she suggested with a mock huskiness and a furious batting of her eyelashes that he couldn't possibly interpret as alluring.

'One is important to you,' he said softly. 'You said you wouldn't give this particular man up—'

'I'm floored by your dogged persistence. Give it a rest.'

'Don't you want a loving husband and children?' he asked quietly.

'The men I meet seem to confuse lust with love,' she said wryly.

'You actually know the difference?' he mocked.

Her eyes became a smoky blue and she twiddled her fork aimlessly on her plate. 'I know. Love is when I look at someone and can't speak for the feelings inside me,'

she said huskily. 'When I care for their needs more than
my own. When I'm blissfully happy with them and half
a person without them. When he's my friend and I feel
that I need no one else in the world.'

She'd said too much. Forcing her appetite to revive,
she packed her fork with fish and tried valiantly to munch
her way through it. Julio had reduced her from an out-
wardly confident, strong woman totally in control of herself, to a weak-kneed eyelash-flutterer with terminal heart
failure and a knotted stomach.

She still loved him. When she looked at him, he filled
the world and she found it hard to look away even for a
moment. Given a little time together, chatting and ex-
changing opinions, they could be friends and lovers again
without effort.

If he weren't married.

Julio's comment was drowned as the loud-speakers
above began to vibrate with the sound of flamenco music—real flamenco, not the sanitised tourist tunes but the
hoarse, heart-wrenching passion of Andalucían gypsies
expressing themselves in raw, throaty song.

Listening, her blood unwillingly fired by the savage
emotions, she nibbled the tapas while Julio sat quietly
beside her. Quiet, but eloquent. Close, but not touching.
Near enough to see the glint in his eyes, to feel the fierce
sexual heat that poured from his body.

The barman placed a plate of asparagus tips between
them and Julio reached for one. Randall's intensely blue
eyes widened as she watched him carefully coat the tip in
butter and then transfer it to his mouth. Her own lips
parted with his and she drew in a sharp breath at the
incredibly sensual way he sucked the asparagus into his
mouth.

'Want some?' he asked softly.

She shook her head with a slow, languorous movement.
And sat frozen with the shame of elemental wanting while
he licked the butter from thumb and forefinger before re-

peating the process, slowly, deliberately enticing her, his mouth buttery and glistening.

The music seemed louder, almost inside her body. Julio shifted on the bar stool, his dark lashes fluttering up indolently. But his eyes told her how the inflammatory music had stirred him deep inside too, heating his smouldering passions to fever-pitch. And she felt swamped by the undercurrents of sensuality in his long, slow look.

The unbearable tension between them seemed to turn her body into a fluid. However much she tried to avoid his eyes, their glances kept colliding, and each time the turbulence between them increased and the hungry sensations in her body became more overwhelming despite her attempts to ignore them.

He said nothing, but sat there devouring her with his gaze, and she felt an excitement that was raw and tantalising like the music, every inch of her aware of him, the broad shoulders, the deep chest, his hands idly playing with the stem of his glass. The curve of his brow, the dark ardour of his compelling eyes...

She swallowed, cocooned, it seemed, in a totally private world where nothing existed other than Julio, not even the noise, the music, the hot-wine aroma from her sizzling prawn dish.

There was a serious intensity about his expression as he slowly lifted a hand and touched the side of her face. A mere butterfly touch—but Randall shivered in her breath at the pleasure it aroused in her body, her eyes startled and bewildered by her extreme reaction to something so simple.

Julio's lips parted and she felt the shaft of desire that went through him because it was arrowing through her too, torturing her with a delicious pain, reminding her again that he was untouchable, unavailable. Spoken for.

Upset, she tried to break the threads that tied them together, to escape from the dangerous way he was scattering her senses and driving her half crazy. It was a frightening power he possessed: the ability to reach inside her body and cause its deepest rhythms to beat so hard that she was oblivious of anything else. No other man made her want to abandon her fiercely held beliefs in the sanctity of marriage and ask for nothing more than to be in his company.

Holding her gaze, he picked up the chit for the tapas and slid from his stool, taking her hand in his. As if in a dream, she followed him to the cash desk, waited in a daze while he paid, and then let him guide her outside.

They walked back to the car park, Randall incapable of rational thought. He was holding her hand with tenderness as he had in the old days, strolling unhurriedly, their hips brushing every now and then with a contact that set her on fire.

There was no pavement beneath her feet, no people thronging the streets for the evening stroll, the *paseo*. It wasn't real, what they were doing. It wasn't real because it was the dream she'd nursed for years; she and Julio, reunited in love, happily hand in hand together. And he was acting it out so perfectly that she was spellbound with the painful joy of it all.

By the car, he gently lifted both her hands and kissed her palms with a deep, passionate concentration of his lowered eyes that made her heart skip a beat. Somehow, despite her protests, he'd placed her arms around his neck, somehow his face was close, his fingers threading through her hair.

'Randall...' he whispered with an infinite, heartbreaking sadness. His lips touched her temples, feeling, she knew, the heavy beat of each deep pulse. She lifted her face languidly to refuse him, swaying in her dream. Through her half-opened eyes, she could see how fiercely he was controlling himself.

She wanted his kiss. Wanted it with a devouring violence of passion that frightened her. 'Julio...' was all she could say.

His tongue licked the corner of her mouth and her lips parted treacherously. But he was inhaling the scent of her hair and his hoped-for kiss never came. There was a delicate touch—was there? She wasn't sure—that electrified the hardening centre of each breast. They lifted provocatively and he groaned. 'God!' he said, his voice thick with desire.

Slowly, as she watched, hypnotised, his forefinger slid into his mouth and then he was drawing its wetness down the line of her cleavage as far as her dress would allow, while she stood there quite paralysed with sensation, too weak, too washed with the insanity of her dream to stop him. Down went his head and she waited in an agony of anticipation for the touch of his lips.

Instead, he blew gently.

'Ohhhh!' she whimpered, her eyes bolting wide open in shock at the contraction of her stomach and loins, almost as if he'd hit her there with his fist.

'More?' And he lightly ran his tongue over the high swell of each breast, gently drew back her neckline a little and blew again on the wet skin, reducing her to a shuddering, quivering wanton.

'Julio, no!' she moaned, wanting to beg him to kiss her, but prevented by her feebly fading voice.

Close by, a car started up, penetrating her conscious mind. And her conscience. Randall came at last to her senses though nothing would make her body obey her wish to move back out of harm's way.

'I…' She thoroughly moistened her lips and tried again. 'You must stop. I've—got—to go,' she said thickly, finding each word an extraordinary effort.

'Of course,' he murmured. To her surprise, he stepped back and for a moment she thought he was quite cold and unmoved by all that had happened, till she felt—even from the distance now separating them—the ebb and flow of his heated breath on her sensitised mouth. And there in the depths of his burning eyes she saw a yearning beyond that of lust that tugged at her heart and left her feeling confused and distressed.

'I—I'll be off, then,' she mumbled, quivering as his limpid gaze fastened hungrily on to her parched lips. 'Thank you for the drink,' she croaked, as if the exquisite torment had never occurred.

He gave a faint smile. 'My pleasure,' he said in a muted growl.

With difficulty she started the truck. Backing it in the confined space, her mind fuzzy as if she'd drunk a bottle of champagne, she hit the wall with a jarring thud. 'Stupid!' she seethed, including her indecent urges and her terrible driving in one fell swoop.

She wouldn't look at Julio in case he was laughing. Man triumphant. '*Idiot*!' Fuming at her unbelievable behaviour, she clamped her trembling hands around the steering-wheel till they hurt and jammed her foot on the accelerator, lurching forwards in a series of kangaroo hops.

Away from the distraction of his ink-dark eyes, she managed to get on to the road without hitting anything else. She didn't want to think about her behaviour, only to drive back to her cottage, bolt the door and draw all the curtains. She needed privacy.

She groaned. She needed protection from herself. An old-fashioned duenna would do, so she could conduct her meetings with Julio through iron bars.

Anyone watching would have imagined she was a learner driver. With elaborate, almost drunken care, she trundled slowly back over the bridge and through the old town. Soon she was out in the country again, her hands still fiercely clenching the wheel, her teeth jammed together and her eyes staring ahead in fierce concentration.

A goat hurtled into the road and she slammed on her brakes to avoid it. The truck stalled. 'That's the last straw!' she wailed, after several attempts to start it again.

She leapt down and heaved up the bonnet, her jitters

heightened by the fact that Julio was sitting behind her in his car, one arm draped casually out of his open window. Nerves made her clumsy. She checked the electrics, half her attention on the clunking sound of a heavy car door, the light tread of feet on tarmac, the unmistakable pressure in the air that skimmed over her back every time Julio came near her.

'Would you like me to check it over?' he asked politely, as though they were total strangers.

'I think it's a hospital case,' she said, attempting a joke and thinking that she was in need of treatment, too. In a mental hospital. She ducked out from under the bonnet and managed a wry smile that would have fooled no one.

'Hold these.' Julio shrugged off his jacket and flicked out the cufflinks then rolled his sleeves up. Randall shifted from one foot to another, feeling awkward and embarrassed. 'Try it.' She did. Nothing. The engine was lifeless. 'You'll have to abandon it,' he frowned. 'It needs a complete overhaul.'

'I know,' she said gloomily. 'We can't afford it.'

'I'll take you back.'

She wouldn't look at him. Intent on her feet, she debated the wisdom of driving in close confinement with Julio after what had happened in public. Her body ignited as it dawned on her that in the bar they had virtually been making silent, distant love.

'You could ring a garage—' she croaked.

'Don't be silly, Randall,' he said quietly. 'Your truck is beyond a simple repair. You can't stay here, out on the open road at this time of the evening. Get in. I'll put your stuff in the boot.'

'I don't trust you,' she muttered.

'Very wise,' he said disarmingly.

She blinked, exasperated, biting her lip with indecision. 'You won't touch me?' she mumbled.

His eyes mocked her remorselessly. 'I don't need to,' he answered callously, with total justification.

He could make love at forty paces, she thought morosely, heat her up slowly to boiling point, let her simmer till she'd been softened all the way through and was ready to be devoured.

'I'd rather take my chances here for the night,' she grated.

'I can't allow that.' Julio sounded stern. 'My honour would never permit—'

'Your honour?!' she gasped, quite beside herself with the emotions that tore at her. 'It's very convenient, this honour of yours! It comes and goes, according to what you want to do! Heavens, the thought of leaving a woman alone on the road to a possible fate worse than death is quite out of the question!' she scathed. 'But slyly seducing her yourself is fine! Is this what you have in mind on the way back? A stop-over somewhere dark and private? A tumble in the back seat, maybe?' she croaked, torturing herself. 'You're *married*!' she raged. 'Married! Where is your honour? Where—?'

'She's dead.'

Randall froze at Julio's cold, unemotional words. Her eyes searched his, seeking the truth. And he was serious, the bitterness in the lines of his face quite awful to see. Her hand flew to her mouth in horror. 'Dead?' she whispered.

'I thought you'd forgotten I was married,' he said coldly. 'That's how it looked to me. Get in the car.'

She reddened. 'It's—it's impossible! She—'

'I was *there*, for God's sake!' he snarled.

'I'm sorry,' she said unhappily, feeling his pain acutely. 'I meant—she was so young...when—?'

'A month after our wedding,' he said savagely, as though resenting the cruelty of fate.

Randall gasped. Cruel indeed. For all three of them. He'd lost his young bride, Elvira had died before she could enjoy her marriage and...a small moan escaped Randall's pale lips. Julio had no feelings for her at all, or he would surely have returned to seek her out. Yet she could only feel pity for him now, deprived of the child-bride he'd evidently adored, the aristocratic girl he'd married so abruptly. No duty marriage, then. It had been a love-match and she could find it in her heart to forgive him that.

'The…the papers splashed your marriage all over the gossip columns,' she said quietly, controlling her own misery. 'She—she was very young. How…what happened, Julio?'

'Leave it,' he muttered.

'I'm sorry,' she said softly. 'I don't want to hurt you with memories.'

A great juddering sigh went through his body. 'Now will you get in?'

'Well, I…' She hesitated uncertainly, but there was no sexual menace in him any more. He looked like a snarling, wounded tiger, too caught up in his own anguish to be concerned about anything else. 'Yes. Of course,' she said mechanically, pushing away the longing to comfort him. 'I'll accept your offer, and thank you.'

Without a word, he opened the car door and she dipped down to the low, luxurious kid leather seat. The car was quite simply breathtaking. Low and mean and growling. Like Julio, she mused.

He drove confidently, beautifully, with a soft, sighing love-song playing on the cassette that Randall tried her best to ignore. She stared out at the olive groves, wondering about Elvira's premature death, and saw that the crumpled-tissue petals of the cistus bushes were dropping to leave room for the next day's quota of flowers. It was all so beautiful and yet it added to her sadness.

Not surprisingly, neither of them spoke a word, and she assumed that Julio was as taken up with thinking about Elvira as she was. Driving up to the car park in front of Santini's mansion, he surprised her by heavily revving the powerful engine and slamming a fist repeatedly on the horn.

Randall jerked her head around, startled. 'Why did you do that?!' she said irritably. 'You'll get Don Carlos out of bed! He'll be furious with me!'

Julio eyed her strangely. 'I'm sure he will,' he said menacingly, trapping her with his hands on either side of the seat. 'This is to make a statement. Just in case my cousin has any feelings of ownership towards you and on the off-chance that he *is* your mysterious lover.'

'What statement?' she whispered, wary of his glittering eyes.

'This one.' He caught her shoulders in rough, brutal hands and drove his mouth into hers hard.

She fought strongly, pinned by his weight. 'Julio! Whatever do you think—?'

His tongue speared warm and erotic into her mouth and she shuddered through the length of her body. Her hands were grasping his hair, tugging with all their strength till she thought she'd tear it out at the roots.

He resisted. And she felt herself alarmingly close to enjoying the shockingly sexual kiss: the teasing flicker of his tongue, the urgent rhythmical breathing that shimmered on her skin and the slow, mesmeric movement of his hands rotating on her shoulders when all the time she wanted them to...

She heaved violently on his hair and was free. 'You brute!' she said hoarsely, wiping her mouth with the back of her hand. Her eyes glimmered with unshed tears of humiliation. 'You unfeeling, vicious brute!' she wailed, and fumbled hysterically with the seatbelt.

He undid it for her, his whole body tense. 'I think,' he said softly, 'I have successfully made my claim.'

'What...claim?' she forced out thickly.

'I want you,' he growled. 'Even if I hate you, loathe you, despise you, it doesn't seem to make any difference. But I have every intention of having you before long and you have no choice in the matter. I thought my cousin should know.'

Aghast, she followed the jerk of Julio's dark head. Beneath the porch stood Carlos Santini, white with shock and as immovable as a statue.

Randall felt she could have cheerfully strangled Julio; slowly, with feeling. 'You worm!' she cried angrily. 'You—oh, God, I wish I had a vocabulary of swear words to let loose on you! You know what you've done, don't you?'

'Made your lover jealous?' he suggested.

'No! You've probably lost me my job,' she seethed. 'And it was the best thing that's happened to me for ages!'

'Not a very good comment on your exciting life of hedonistic pleasure,' he drawled.

'I'm going to count to ten,' she said grimly. 'And you're going to disappear in a puff of smoke. Then I'll be given an award for not taking an axe to your neck even under extreme provocation.'

'Finished counting yet?' he murmured.

'It's a nightmare,' she told herself calmly.

'No, no,' he mocked, patting her knee with a proprietorial air. 'This is real. I've just made the two of you aware that I'm determined to make love to you, Randall.'

'You need locking up!' she spluttered. 'I'll be no one's one-night stand—'

'I should hope not! I was expecting a little more than that,' he said lazily.

'I'd dearly love to take you for a walk near a stack of manure and push you in!' she raged.

'I think this violence of yours is promising,' remarked Julio with infuriating smugness. 'Don't worry about it, though,' he murmured. 'We'll channel your aggression properly when you're in my bed.'

'I'm surprised you haven't called a lackey to have me washed and brought to your tent,' she said sarcastically. 'I'm not up for grabs, short- or long-term. I can accept that you're frustrated but you said yourself that there's no future in a relationship between people like us—'

'That's true. But when I said that, I was referring to you and him,' Julio explained.

She blinked in horror. 'Me and...' Following the jerk of Julio's head, she saw that Santini was banging on Julio's window angrily and she hadn't even noticed. 'Oh! I could die!' she wailed. 'I always end up being humiliated by you! Let me out you brute, or so help me, I'll smash a window!'

'Reinforced glass. You'd break the bones in your hand,' he informed her maliciously.

However, as she drew in breath to yell at him she heard the click of the locks and she wrenched at the handle, half falling out and meeting Santini's horrified eyes above the low roof of the car.

'Don Carlos!—I'm sorry... I—I didn't—' she began jerkily, her face the colour of scarlet poppies.

Santini swore at Julio with a bitterness that astonished her. There were undercurrents between the two men she didn't understand. Despite his slender build, Santini was so incensed that when Julio slid out of the car he grasped Julio's lapels, standing on tiptoe to hurl insults at his cousin.

Julio remained ice-cold and composed, only the glint in his eyes betraying the anger he felt at Santini's invective. Slowly, with the utmost contempt, he uncurled his cousin's fingers from his jacket.

'This one's mine,' he said with chilling confidence.

'Oh, no, she's *not*!' snapped Randall furiously.

Santini's eyes flickered. 'You...reject Julio's advances?' he said in amazement.

'Of course I do!' she seethed, glowering at the impassive Julio. 'He deliberately did that to provoke you and make life impossible for me!'

'My dear,' sympathised Don Carlos. 'I think you need

my protection. You don't seem safe in that cottage after all. Perhaps you should come and live in the house—'

'I'll ring my sister,' said Julio coldly.

'No!' Carlos hastily composed himself. 'Her tour mustn't be interrupted. How selfish of you!' he declared reprovingly.

'I think it's time your face was remodelled,' reflected Julio in a sinister tone. 'Leave Randall alone or I'll cause such trouble—'

'I'm sure she'd feel safer with me than you,' muttered Santini. 'We have shared confidences already, haven't we, Randall?'

She stared at him in dismay. Surely he wasn't going to reveal her secret? 'I—we've chatted,' she admitted feebly.

Santini smiled in satisfaction but she was more aware of Julio's indrawn breath. 'She doesn't want you, Julio,' he said triumphantly, holding out his hand invitingly to Randall. 'I'm the one she trusts with her intimate secrets.'

'You've been very kind,' said Randall stiffly, ignoring the hand. This was beginning to look like a gladiatorial contest with her as the prize. Whatever was going on between these two men? How dared they use her to establish their wretched macho sexual supremacy over each other! 'I must get my groceries in before the butter melts,' she grated. 'Excuse me.'

'The bags are heavy. You'll need some help,' murmured Julio.

'No. I don't,' she said firmly.

'Looks as if you have enough for two,' said Santini meaningfully and, furious with him for thinking this was a game, she telegraphed a warning with her eyes.

'I hope you two weren't planning a midnight feast, like naughty children in the dorm,' drawled Julio. His eyes glittered and his next words were like cutting steel. 'I'd be forced to punish you both if I found you together.'

Randall felt like yelling. 'Don't *pester* me!' she wailed and stormed around to the car boot, struggling with the awkward, heavy bags. Although she could barely carry them, she was determined to make a martyr of herself and wild horses wouldn't make her give them up to one of the hovering men.

'Stubborn woman,' Julio said softly and she scowled because it was true. 'I'll get a mechanic to your truck in the morning,' he called after her as she staggered grimly down the path, wondering if her arms would be wrenched from their sockets.

Turning and delivering a filthy look in his direction, Randall said bitterly, 'It's the least you can do!'

'There's more to come,' he answered. 'Prepare yourself.'

'Oh, God!' she whispered to herself. There would be no peace till he had what he wanted. And at the moment it seemed he wanted her. She stared at him, trembling, then her eyes swivelled to Santini and she knew from his expression that he meant to use his knowledge about Tom to his own advantage. The Quadra men seemed determined to seduce her and she was vulnerable to both.

CHAPTER SIX

IN A T-shirt and shorts the colour of foxgloves, and keeping her eyes open for either of the two men, Randall wearily began work in Santini's garden the next day. She'd spent an edgy night waiting for something to happen and a miserably lonely breakfast-time wishing she could be with Tom.

As her hand hovered over a rampant clump of thyme that had sprawled merrily across the gravel path she thought that the days ahead seemed like an eternity. Could she spend *any* time away from her son? They'd been so close up to now. She hadn't realised how much of her life meshed with his. The fun they had together each morning before she went to work and he'd gone to Ana had always brightened her heart and set her up for the day.

She glared at the cause of her troubles, lounging in an all-white outfit on the terrace beneath a striped awning, reading, sipping drinks, watching everything she did from under the brim of a panama hat, his eyes hidden by reflective sunglasses.

With some difficulty, Randall struggled to overcome the fact that she missed Tom so badly. Since there was no choice, she could do nothing but put up with the situation and not let Julio get her down—or the worry that Santini was also interested in her. At least this was a beautiful place to work, she mused. Jewelled butterflies were everywhere, clouds of them, and the garden was drenched in fragrance.

The surroundings and the simple pleasures of her work began to help her unwind. Confidence in her own skills here gave her the assurance to deal with Julio if necessary

and it didn't bother her too much when he sauntered over
to supervise more closely.

'Nice action,' he approved, as she bent and slashed at
some woody lavender bushes.

'I'm good with a knife,' she said drily. 'I wouldn't
come too close. I've been known to get carried away.'

'Sounds thrilling,' he commented.

'Depends whether you like air vents in your trousers or
not,' she retorted sweetly.

When the bushes had been tamed, Randall turned her
attention to neatening the camomile path, taking a delight
in the mat of cushioned green and the wonderful scents
she released when she began to trim it. Her eyes caught
sight of a blue-spotted lizard. It was lurking on a flat stone
and beadily eyeing a swallowtail butterfly. Before she
could do anything, Julio's hand appeared near her foot
and the lizard scuttled away.

'Pity all predators aren't so easy to scare off,' he said
enigmatically. She couldn't have agreed with him more.

Gently he coaxed the butterfly to safety without harm-
ing its delicate wings or the hair-thin legs. At last it fluttered off, unaware that it had narrowly escaped oblivion.
Tom would have been thrilled, she thought wistfully.

'You always were good with animals,' she said grudg-
ingly, wishing he'd display the same kindness towards
her.

When he stood up again, he smiled the smile that had
always made her heart turn over. It obliged again. 'Do
you remember the tawny owl?' he reminisced. 'The one
with the injured wing?'

Randall's face softened. It was a story she'd told Tom
many times and she'd recognised Julio's love for animals
in her child's shining eyes. 'You got a rocket when they
found your bed empty on the night we took the owl into
the wood and watched it fly away,' she remembered.

Julio shrugged. 'It was worth it.'

The memory was too strong not to be enjoyed. It had

been wonderful, seeing the owl flap silently off and disappear. 'I felt a shiver down my back,' she said softly, 'when we heard its mate calling—'

'Yes,' murmured Julio. 'And you hugged me so tightly I thought I'd never breathe again.' His hand drifted down her bare arm and she stiffened. 'You have that effect on me still, Randall,' he said, his voice low and caressing. 'That breathlessness inside me whenever you're near. And deny it if you will, but we could be very close once more if—'

'We *were* close, Julio, but you didn't realise the special relationship we had. If you'd only come to tell me honestly that you didn't care for me, I might have come to terms with the fact that you'd fallen in love with another woman. But you—'

'I did what I had to do,' he said quietly. 'I behaved as I did for the good of my family. Sometimes you have to make choices, Randall. Maybe you will, one day—something will force you to make a choice between the two things you want most in the world.' He paused, thought better of what he had planned to say and turned on his heel to stride quickly away.

Randall reflected on what he'd said. Elvira had evidently been ill—perhaps terminally ill, even before they married. Although he'd fallen in love with his young wife, he might have agreed to marry her out of pity. He was like that—or had been—sacrificing himself for just causes. Twice to her knowledge he'd taken the blame for something another boy had done. Those boys would have been denied weekend leave, and Julio knew their divorcee mothers looked forward to the company of their sons.

She chewed her lip thoughtfully. Julio had always defended the weak and supported his family. For that, she couldn't fault him. Perhaps she'd judged him too hastily.

During the course of the morning, he kept appearing, chatting and passing comment. Frequently she wanted to respond to his questions and explain what she was doing and why, because she knew he was genuinely interested. Yet wisely she kept silent, head down, stubbornly refusing to respond.

That was like a red rag to a fighting bull. He unleashed the full force of his charm on her, which was worse. When the razor thorns of a thick bramble whipped into the back of her knee, he showed such concern on his face and in his voice that she felt her heart-rate accelerating dangerously and knew she was risking trouble. Somehow she had to get rid of him.

'What are you doing?' she asked him crossly, gingerly trying to free herself.

'Kneeling.' He clasped her ankle and held it rigid. 'Don't move.' Gently he reached around her leg and eased the bramble free. Then his palm slid over her smooth skin to where she could feel a little blood trickling down. 'I'd better clean this up a little,' he said, looking up at her, his eyes smouldering unfairly.

'I don't need—ohhh!' she cried in shock. His mouth was warm and moist on the sensitive flesh, gently licking, and a million volts seemed to be shooting through her body. 'Let me go!' she grated furiously, ineffectually trying to pull her leg away from his iron grip.

'Delicious,' he pronounced, suddenly standing up. 'Won't your lover be annoyed!'

'Is that what you're doing?' she snapped. 'Pretending to make a play for me to annoy Don Carlos? Heavens, Julio! Your cousin isn't jealous of me, so you can stop this pantomime at once!'

He laughed as she stomped off racking her brains for a way to drive him indoors and give her see-sawing emotions time to settle down. With a pile of dry foliage to dispose of, she suddenly had an idea. A wicked smile lit her face and she checked the direction of the wind. A bonfire! Marching back and forth across the lawn, she deposited all the dry herbage in a heap and set fire to it.

Smoke drifted in Julio's direction and he looked up

from where he had settled himself to drink some sweet, fresh lemon. Then the full blast of blazing sage bushes reached his nostrils. He rose and calmly took his chair across the lawn out of the smoke-line. Inspired, she began to mow, the noise of the ride-on mower shattering the peace beautifully.

'Mind your feet!' she yelled, hurtling in top gear towards his chair.

'You're playing merry hell with the straight lines!' he bellowed as she chugged past, and leapt out of the way just in time.

'I'm designing a Chinese logo,' she shouted in satisfaction. OK, it was stupid, she thought. But it afforded her a lot of pleasure!

As she headed back towards him, Julio gave her a sardonic look and moved again to the edge of the shrubbery while she busily trundled up and down, making a terrible noise, grating the gears alarmingly. At last, unable to stand the racket any longer, he stood in front of the mower. She contemplated running him over but couldn't bring herself to do so.

So she turned off the engine and removed her earmuffs. 'Yes?' she enquired with insincere, humble deference.

'Stop mowing,' he ordered lazily. 'I think you've said something very rude in Mandarin.'

Although she managed to stop a laugh, her eyes treacherously sparkled with amusement. 'But I'm in the middle of this really pretty criss-cross pattern,' she protested innocently.

'There'll be a pretty criss-cross pattern on your rear if you continue,' he retorted.

'Oh, dear! This is terribly awkward,' she gushed. 'Don Carlos asked me to do the lawn today. What will I tell him?' she fluttered in mock alarm.

'That I forced you to stop because you'd offended the owners of the local Chinese take-away who were passing by,' said Julio sardonically, not at all fooled by her Sweet Innocence act. 'And that I threatened to throw a brick beneath the cutters.'

'Such violence! They say it's due to an excess of testosterone,' she confided.

Julio's eyes glittered. 'Could be an excess of your sauce making a few things hard to swallow.'

Her gurgle of explosive laughter made him grin but the look in his eyes told her that she'd gone far enough so she decided to retire gracefully. 'Awful, being thwarted,' she sympathised, unable to resist that last taunt. 'Makes you choke on your fortune cookies, doesn't it? Very well, sir,' she continued demurely. 'I'll stop since the victory is mine.'

His mouth twitched and she grinned irrepressibly back at the blank dark glasses. 'Careful,' he murmured huskily. 'I might find your defiance a challenge to my masculinity—and rise to it.'

A deep blush swept over her face at his suggestive expression and she quickly turned away, thinking of other ways of getting rid of him. Like a lord, he reclined in a luxurious wicker lounger, shifting his body contentedly on the plump cushions till he was comfortable and had thought up his next round of wicked remarks to confound her again.

Two could play at being provocative. She had noisy machines on her side. Collecting ropes and a chainsaw, she clanked a metal ladder past the shrubbery and leaned it against a huge chestnut tree which had several dead branches. Safely up in the canopy, she could see him watching with interest as she swung like a female Tarzan on the rope from branch to branch. And then, slipping on her ear muffs, she started the chainsaw up and began to lop the branches, letting them thud to the ground with what must be a highly satisfying sound.

A little while later, as she was assembling ropes on the spacious junction of four branches, a hand came from behind and lifted her ear muffs and a strong arm stole around her body to steady her, correctly anticipating her start of surprise.

'Heavens! How did you get up here?' she asked stupidly, trying to force a gap between her spine and his chest.

'Easily. I've come to surrender,' Julio said huskily in her ear.

She quelled the tremor that threatened to ripple through her. 'Oh, good. How much of a surrender?' she asked hopefully.

'All the way.'

Alarmed, she ducked down swiftly, slipping from his arms and turned, giving him a wary look. 'You're tired of annoying me and trying to make out I'm digging gold out of Don Carlos and you're going home?' she asked, wondering why on earth the prospect made her mouth want to turn down.

'No,' he said, deceptively amiable. 'But I'll leave you alone for a couple of hours if you'll stop trying to break the decibel record.'

He grinned, so beautifully that she hastily thought of something crushing for her own sanity. 'You're ruining your dazzling Marks and Sparks outfit,' she remarked insultingly.

'It's an Alvarado, and nothing, certainly not my clothes, will stop me climbing up for what I want,' he said with soft menace. 'Is it a deal?'

'And if it isn't?' she asked stupidly.

'Oh, I'll show you how to make love in a tree,' he said huskily, hauling her against him. 'First you have to make sure you're quite secure—' She gasped. He'd deftly slipped the rope around her arms, pinning them to her sides. 'Then,' he said, smiling broadly at her, 'you start undoing buttons—'

'It's a deal!' she croaked, unnervingly helpless to stop him.

'Pity. It was beginning to enjoy the remake of Tarzan and Jane. This would make a perfect site for a tree-house, too. We could have a lot of fun up here,' he murmured confidentially.

'I see the ape,' she retorted huskily, deciding to go down fighting. 'Where's Tarzan?'

Julio gave a wolfish, predatory smile. 'Can't tell the difference? Tarzan's the one with smooth skin on his body. Let me show you,' he offered, turning his attention to his own buttons. Mesmerised, she watched each one being slipped free to reveal the gleaming oak of his torso, the achingly finger-touchable skin stretched taut and firm over his rib-cage.

Gorgeous, she thought in awe, her own chest tightening. 'We—we made a deal,' she murmured, unnervingly defenceless suddenly and trying in vain to unglue her eyes from the magnificence of his body. But all she could do was to imagine her palms flat on the warm skin and the wonderful sensation there would be of a softly cloaked strength.

'Shame that it's a deal I can't honour,' he said ruthlessly, his eyes virtually scorching the clothes from her body.

'Oh.' That was honest. Too honest. She worried about his hovering fingers inches from her breasts. 'Me Jane. Not the ape. You don't have to check.'

'But sorting out who we are and what we want is only the start,' he said softly. He stretched out a hand and it came to rest on the swell of her hip, his eyes—and hers—following its gentle rotation. 'I believe they cohabited for years.'

'Who did?' she mumbled, wanting to close her eyes on the lyrical wash of pleasure that his hand was arousing inside her.

'Tarzan and Jane,' he murmured. 'I suppose they started somewhere. Shall we begin? Uh…here, maybe?' His fingers slid into the warmth of her thigh and lightly walked down, down, down… Randall drew in a shuddery breath when Julio knelt and ardently began to kiss her knees.

'Why—are you—doing this to me?' she jerked. He paused briefly, his lips hot and moist on the inside of her leg. Rising, she thought in alarm, very slowly but surely upwards. Towards… 'Offside rule!' she whimpered.

'Wrong sport. I'm invoking *noviesca*,' he said silkily, his hands slipping up the backs of her thighs.

'What—?' She tried to move sideways. His hands tightened and held her fast, his lips tasting her smooth golden skin with such agonisingly sweet pleasure that she felt as if her body had been liquidised, and put on an open fire to steam.

'What's *noviesca*?' he supplied obligingly. But huskily, she noticed, her legs beginning to tremble, as though there was the same turbulence inside him too.

The crawl of his fingers inched paralysingly up and met the lower swell of her buttocks beneath her shorts. 'I'm being assaulted from all sides,' she moaned in protest.

'That's right,' he agreed hoarsely, his tongue slicking up the salt on her firm upper thigh.

The gentle pressure on her buttocks as he explored was making her eyes close at last. Ridiculous, she thought wildly, incapable of understanding how that could happen when her eyes and her rear were in different parts of her body. 'I'll yell for reinforcements,' she husked weakly.

'The Tarzan mating call? Everyone's out. And I don't think you could, anyway,' he murmured, infuriatingly *right*.

'Please, Julio, don't use me like this!' she moaned.

'I'm allowed. That's *noviesca*. I'll tell you about it when I'm not so busy. I'm a little preoccupied right now.'

She looked down on his dark head, her hands clenching and unclenching impotently. She wanted to grab a handful of the raven hair and tear it from his scalp. She wanted to throw him off the tree… 'Ohhh!' she whispered. Julio was nuzzling her pelvis and even beneath the cotton shorts she could feel the warmth of his mouth, the rasping heat of his breath, the hard pressure of his chin, jaw, nose, as they moved inexorably towards the place where the molten pulses were driving her wild.

Her hands tried to stretch out to him. Throw him off the tree? No. She wanted to catch his head and force it harder into her body to ease the ache. She wanted... 'Oh, dear God!' she mouthed, utterly appalled at her abandoned thoughts.

Slowly, painfully, Julio staggered to his feet. And now she dearly wanted to rail at him for stopping. But she kept her teeth clenched, dismayed by the violence he aroused in her.

Julio seemed to be having a hard time speaking. He licked his lips, briefly closed his drugged eyes and caught her face in his hands, kissing her so hard that her whole body braced in response. 'Randall,' he growled. 'Now I have you and I won't let you go. I will lock you in a room and come to you a thousand times a day, arousing you inch by inch until you beg me to make love to you. I want you,' he husked, accompanying his words with head-spinning kisses. 'I will have you, naked, waiting for me. Opening your arms...your whole body, to me.'

She felt the hard ridge of his hip against hers, then the harder, hotter flame of male virility that leapt and burnt with shocking urgency between their two bodies. He shifted his hips and she let out a small whimper as her body contracted in readiness. And he began to loosen the rope, then silently, a little clumsily, undid each of the small buttons down the front of her bright top while she did nothing to stop him.

His breathing rasped her throat, heavy and rhythmical. Dazed, she tipped her head back to expose the maximum of skin to it. There was the sweetness of his lips sliding along her jaw and then covering every inch of her neck. And the warmth of his hands covering the lacy cups of her half-bra, his eyes… She quivered as her heart stopped, lurched and recovered itself. His eyes gazed with intense awe on the lush upswell of her breasts and she felt bewildered that his admiration should give her such an intensely profound satisfaction.

'God, you're so gorgeous I could eat you,' he said in a soft, covetous growl.

'You will,' she moaned apprehensively.

He gave a sinister chuckle and her hands lifted to his shoulders, intending to push him away. Instead she found that her hands had accidentally moved beneath the material of his shirt. Just for a moment, her fingers lingered; only briefly, she told herself, placating her conscience. She was gathering strength to repel him and then she'd snap him out of this with a few well-chosen words. When she could think of some.

Blue eyes met darkly smouldering brown. He was flinching, shuddering and she looked down in surprise to see that she was lightly trailing the tips of her fingers over his skin, which felt wonderfully luxurious. Sensual, like a rich fabric. And yes, like iron beneath. But warm. Fascinated, she forgot everything but the sensation beneath her fingertips.

Her palms shaped the well-developed planes of his chest, an exploratory finger reaching out tentatively to the dark nipples. Julio shuddered and groaned. Hazily she lifted her head from her contemplation of his body. One of his big hands clamped on her bottom and pushed her hard against him again to make her aware of the extent of his arousal. Hotter, harder than before.

She bit her lip hard, knowing that she must never surrender to his seduction. Resentment of this fact made her angry. She wanted him so acutely that she could hardly bear it. Why couldn't she be like a man, and have a clear conscience about casual sex? Except this wasn't casual for her, she acknowledged reluctantly. She was being seduced by the man she loved.

'Set me free,' she pleaded in a husky whisper, and wished she could be free from love and its pain. She knew so surely that love had the power to tear her in two.

'I'm not holding you a prisoner,' he murmured, scattering her upturned face with kisses.

You are, you are! she wanted to yell. 'Step back,' she mumbled.

He did. But the heat between them still pulsed into her body, scattering her senses. And his fingers had dipped into the froth of lace around her breasts and gently curved beneath each one, lifting them to his avid gaze.

'So soft, smooth...' His thumbs grazed her hard, lifting nipples which looked as dark as bruised fruit, and they tightened, sending a fan of tingling sensation into the corners of her body. 'Responsive...' His eyes dilated. 'Luscious,' he said thickly, his head angling down.

'No, don't— Mmm!' she squeaked, silenced. One plum-dark peak lay surrounded by warmth and she felt a gentle pull as he tugged with his lips and then took it deeper into his mouth, suckling so intently that her emotions became confused with the image of Tom, sweet, black-lashed and content, and Julio, dangerous, hungry, but infinitely beautiful as he nursed at her breast. The two men she loved... One in danger. *Tom.* 'I can't...oh, please stop!' she trembled.

His head lifted. Her left breast seemed deprived, aching for the feel of his mouth. Without thinking, she drew down one of her trembling hands from where it had cradled his head—how had it got there?—and pressed it firmly to herself in compensation. And blushed when she found a hard, thrusting nipple forcing its way between her fingers.

Julio firmly removed her hand and satisfied the throbbing ache. To some extent. She burned. Every inch of her was directed with a crucifying agony towards the focus of her turbulent sexuality.

'Now I know what kept Tarzan in the forest for so

long,' he mocked softly, his mouth moist and sensual from tending to her need. 'I always wondered. The breeze on naked skin, a willing woman—'

'You bastard!' she groaned, feeling cheap. Blindly she struggled without success to dress herself.

'Come here, Randall!' he commanded, seeing her difficulties. 'I'll do it. You're incapable.' He brushed her trembling hands aside.

'Only because I'm angry!' she blazed, furious that he seemed in control. But then his hand accidentally met the deep valley between each provocatively swollen breast and his intake of breath told her otherwise.

'Hell,' he growled, bemused, staring at his fingers as if they'd become fused together.

Randall tried biting her lip and it helped to bring her back to her senses. Slowly, aware of his hot, drowsy and mocking eyes lingering on every movement she made, she managed to bring the lace over her engorged curves and concentrate on the task of making a handful of thumbs work tiny pearlised buttons into place again.

'How ever will I get down from here?' she muttered, knowing her shaking legs wouldn't bear her weight.

'In my arms.' Julio tucked in his shirt with lean fingers and she found herself longingly watching.

'I'd rather jump,' she said unconvincingly.

He gave a knowing, disbelieving smile that made her go pink with shame and then she was pulled into his hard, tense body with a brutal urgency. 'I want you, Randall,' he growled. 'I claim the right to you in the old way because we were once engaged. *That* is *noviesca*.' He looked down on her with a proprietorial air. 'Andalucían custom accepts that a betrothed woman belongs to the man,' he explained. 'If he breaks the engagement, she still belongs to him, for as long as he wishes. So you are mine and I intend to make full use of that fact.'

'That's archaic!' she husked.

He silenced her with a kiss, as soft as a breeze on her

lips, and it was all she could do not to sigh with pleasure
and link her arms around his neck. 'Who cares?' he
growled, his hands creeping down to the small of her back
and over her neat rear. 'It suits my purpose.' His mouth
travelled erotically along the top of her lip and then his
tongue was slipping into the soft, sensitive warmth of her
mouth while she clung to him weakly, trying to find the
strength to escape his embrace. 'Come to bed with me.
We can spend all day and all night making love—'

'No!' she said sharply, wrenching away. 'You betrayed
me when I loved you so much that I thought no feeling
could ever be that intense. I was wrong: hatred can be
equally powerful. I'm no possession. I'm free, indepen-
dent, like the wounded owl, the butterfly, that toad you
rescued from those boys who were stoning it. You
wouldn't treat animals as contemptuously as you treat
me.'

'They needed my protection. You don't. That's the difference. What you need is sex,' he said insolently.

Randall ground her teeth at his arrogance. 'So I might,'
she said defensively, 'but if I want satisfaction, I'll take
it elsewhere!' she snapped defiantly.

'You do and I'll skin your lover alive!' he growled.

'You'd have to find him first,' she said coldly, privately
awed by his jealous fury. 'Help me down. Life in the
jungle has palled.'

He helped her, first lowering the chainsaw on its rope
and then, agonisingly, curling an arm around her waist,
guiding her feet to secure footholds with great care. She
kept brushing up against his chest, his hip, his thigh, feeling the drift of his breath on her neck, her cheek, her ear…

And at last they were down and she sprang back from
his supporting arms as if they were scalding her.

'For heaven's sake, go inside,' she muttered. 'I have a
job to finish.'

'He looked towards the branches she was scowling at.
'You can't. You'll injure yourself.'

Despite her protests, he untied the chainsaw and began cutting the branches into logs. She left him to it, recognising that at least he was releasing some of his sexual frustration by the physical work.

For the whole day she tried to burn up her aggression too, working through the midday heat and ignoring the enviable clink of a fork on a plate and the chink of ice in a glass as Julio took a break and sat beneath the house awning eating a meal.

She wasn't hungry. With the mounting hours, her anger and bitterness increased till she felt like yelling to let off steam. Finally she collected a pick-axe and vented some of her fire on lifting the paving slabs at the far end of the swimming-pool.

Her steady rhythm faltered when Julio appeared. He looked gorgeous, indecently clothed in a minuscule triangle of white material, the lines of his bronzed body more perfect than they had a right to be. After a tantalisingly brief look, she levered up a slab with more brutality than necessary.

But something made her flick another glance in his direction. He stood on the edge of the pool, staring at the still turquoise water as though it held the secrets of the universe, his strong body strangely vulnerable. She looked blindly at the head of her pick, thinking of being in his arms, while he…he thought of what, she wondered?

A polite cough made them both start, look at one another and turn guiltily to a waiting maid. '*Marqués de la Quadra, hay una llamada para usted,*' said the maid politely, holding a portable phone and offering him the receiver.

He frowned. 'For me? Who?' He muttered in irritation. '*Quién es?*' he corrected.

'Buenos Aires,' smiled the maid indulgently. 'Isabel!'

The effect of the name on Julio was magical. A soft expression came over his entire face, washing it with delight…and love. Randall flinched as he gave a happy cry and almost snatched the phone from the maid. '*Querida*...' he murmured. And proceeded to tell the listening Isabella how much he'd missed her.

Horrified by the power of her feelings, Randall didn't stay around to hear much more. She abandoned her pickaxe and went off to clear the leaves and debris from the lawn, and the appalling pain from her heart. Though she failed to do that.

In her ears rang Julio's tender, courteous, loving voice. Seductive. Full of warmth and happiness. Only it hadn't been for her, it had been for Isabel, and the knowledge that he'd tried to proposition her while all along there was a woman he loved in Buenos Aires made her feel furious.

And, she admitted with reluctance, *viciously* jealous. As a result, the grass suffered from the vigorous raking she inflicted on the leaves and she guiltily pressed down the scored soil with her feet afterwards.

Julio came past her with the phone cradled to his ear as lovingly as though it were Isabel's languid hand. She knew the hand would be languid. Not like hers, she scowled, seeing how red and blistered they were. And the ingrained dirt! She felt that once, just once, she'd like to have that fish-tail dress and blow all thoughts of Isabel from Julio's mind.

He went inside and she lost herself in work, thinking of nothing but what she was doing, counting the minutes till she could escape to the normality of being a mother and talking to her beloved son again.

At seven, her day's work was over, and after showering she changed into Tom's favourite blue sundress, intending to spend the rest of the evening with him. That meant escaping Julio's eagle eye. So she climbed out of the side-window, eased her way up a wistaria and over the wall where her newly repaired truck waited. And, slipping off the handbrake, she let it coast down the hill a little way before she dared to start the engine.

It was wonderful to see Tom and exchange news. After

the children were bathed, everyone ate together in a big, noisy family way and it was almost eleven before they'd finished the meal—though that was normal in Spain. Sleepy toddlers had the remains of pastry and strawberries wiped from their mouths and were put down to sleep, she and Ana rocking the little ones and singing a soft lullaby.

Her sanity restored, Randall gently kissed her son goodnight and fell exhausted into a deep sleep beside him, her determination to hold out against Julio revived by the love in her son's eyes.

'Where the hell have you been?!'

'Good morning, Julio.' Randall coolly slammed her truck door shut.

'I said—'

'I heard. But I'm not late for work,' she pointed out, striding to the garden gate.

His hand checked her, bringing her to a halt. 'You will be by the time you get out of that,' he said tightly, indicating her crumpled dress.

'I'm quick—'

'To strip?' he growled. 'You couldn't even wait to do that, could you? That dress looks as if it's survived a tumble in the hay.' He peered more closely. 'Hell! Are those fingermarks?'

They were. Evidence of the children's enthusiastically sticky hugs. 'Forget this once-engaged-always-mine attitude!' she countered frostily. 'My life is my own. I work hard. I'm entitled to play hard, too. Now let me pass. I have a job to do for Don Carlos—'

'For me,' he said tightly, opening the gate for her. 'You're working for me now.'

She whirled to face him and blanched at the smug look of triumph in his eyes. 'What did you say?'

He caught her elbow and pushed her along the path to her cottage. 'Get your working clothes on. I'll tell you later.'

'Tell me now!' she demanded grimly. He took the key from her, opened the door and walked in. 'Well, make yourself at home!' she snapped sarcastically.

'I have every right to,' he answered calmly. 'It's my cottage.' Her mouth dropped open and he smiled faintly. 'It's my house. My land.'

'Yours?!' she gasped.

'Sure. Everything here is mine. Santini is nothing more than my manager. He looks after my estates in Spain.'

'I'll go and see him about this—' Before she could take more than two steps, Julio had placed his body squarely in front of her. She felt scared by his daunting size, his confidence.

'He's gone,' said Julio with malicious pleasure. 'With a little—er—encouragement from me. Gone to join his wife on tour and hold her hand in between arias.'

'*Gone*?' she repeated dully.

'Upset?' He tipped her chin, the same smug smile on his lips.

'I—no!' she snapped, seeing where his mind was taking him. 'Where does that leave me?' she muttered.

'In my power, I'd say,' mocked Julio.

The muscles in her stomach clenched and knotted. She couldn't stay on at the cottage. Not now. He'd eat her alive. Her lovely job! she wailed silently. 'I'll pack,' she said heavily.

'Your old boss would be furious if you walked out of this job,' Julio observed.

'Steve isn't old and he'd understand, if he thought I was being harassed,' she snapped.

'The word ''old'' was used to indicate that he's not your boss any more.'

'He's not…' Randall went deathly pale. 'Who…?' She gulped, the question unasked. It was unthinkable, impossible, but Julio's smirk spoke volumes. An awful foreboding fluttered inside her as she realised that slowly, surely, he was tying her up, roping her to a tree so she couldn't escape.

'You've got it,' Julio murmured with silky pleasure. 'Steve has sold out to me.'

'You're lying,' she said flatly. 'Steve would tell me before he did so—and he'd sell to the devil himself before you!' she added, remembering how angry Steve had been when Julio had deserted her—and how Steve had exploded with anger when she told him that she was carrying Julio's child.

'I made the purchase through an agent. Steve still doesn't know I was the buyer. And he never had time to think, let alone check things out with you,' drawled Julio. 'My agent made him an offer he had to accept at once, or not at all. He rang the contact number you'd given him. Here. My maid said you weren't at home.' His eyes glittered with hard lights. 'Pity you decided to spend the night elsewhere.'

It was unnerving. He was getting rid of any opposition, money no object. *Why*? She quailed at his ruthlessness. 'I'll ring him,' she breathed hoarsely.

'You'll get his answerphone. He's gone to England,' gloated Julio.

'You're lying,' she countered, sure at least of that point. Steve had seen her through her pregnancy, held her newborn baby and taken such an interest in her welfare that they'd become very close, like father and daughter. 'He wouldn't sell and go off like that.'

'Something about a friend dying in a hospice?' said Julio quietly.

And Randall remembered. Steve had been aware that his old friend's health had deteriorated and had warned her that any moment he might have to leave her to cope. 'Oh,' she said limply. 'He's gone.' Steve would be totally taken up with his friend's needs. She couldn't unburden her own worries on him at a time like this. 'You went behind his back,' she said resentfully. 'He'll be furious when he knows you've taken over his business.'

'He'll see it the same way as you do, won't he?' Julio said coldly. 'As a dirty trick. You can get together in a few weeks and agree that it's just the kind of low-down thing I'd do, using my money to buy what I want.'

'You said it,' she scowled. Oh, Steve, she thought. If only you knew!

'Let me run my question past you again,' said Julio with a grimly laboured patience. 'What have you been doing all night?'

'What does it matter what I do out of working hours?' she asked belligerently.

'You're mine to do with as I choose. I don't want any other man touching you. Not Steve, Santini, anyone. So I got rid of them—as I will get rid of any other men in your life. Who were you with?' He strode towards her as though he meant to shake the information out of her.

'Stop there!' she warned, her eyes flashing with anger. 'I was with friends.'

'Their names, addresses?'

'Are private,' she said firmly. 'I won't be bullied! You have no right—'

'I must know if you've been with a man,' he muttered. 'And if you won't tell me, there's only one way to find out.'

Before she could move, he had crossed the space between them, taken her in his arms and begun to kiss her, his mouth gentle and coaxing. And she was gentled and coaxed after a long, long while of keeping her mouth stubbornly clamped together, but grimly stopped herself from releasing a sigh and allowing his kiss to probe deeper.

She was woefully incapable of stopping him, however; he took possession of her body and her emotions, nestling her into his cradling arms and caressing her breast till the sinful heat stole over her and his plundering fingers tossed her body into a languorous excitement. Then he pushed her away, triumph on his face.

'I like your answer,' he said huskily. 'Whatever you did, it wasn't what I feared. Get changed into your work clothes. At lunchtime we'll talk and I'll tell you what changes I'm making.'

She was too choked to argue. With her whole body trembling uncontrollably, she walked blindly into the bedroom and bolted the door before stripping off her dress. The painful peaks of her breasts mocked her. The flush on her body shamed her. When she looked warily in the mirror, she saw what he must have seen; a woman with bed-tumbled hair, enormous indolent eyes beneath half-closed eyelids, and temptingly pouting mouth.

Randall turned from the brazen image of herself in shocked despair. The messages had been there. Julio had only responded as any red-blooded man would, and she didn't know how to keep him or her disturbing need for him at bay any longer.

CHAPTER SEVEN

THAT morning, she worked as hard as she could and then some, thinking reproachfully about Steve's sell-out. Julio swam; she carried out his orders and worked in the pool area, ignoring him—apparently. But she could see him in her mind's eye, cleaving the water, his powerful shoulders gleaming, his forehead slicked with wet curls. Didn't he have any work to do? she wondered crossly. Businesses to buy up, bulls to toss and peasants to sack?

All her energy was expended on energetically heaving the slabs up and 'walking' them to a stack while Julio swam and swam—endlessly, it seemed—the rhythmic slap of water interrupted only by a pause when he produced a racing turn at either end of the pool.

And then her leg was grasped by a wet hand. She stood still, her back to the pool, numbly waiting for his next move.

'We'll eat now.' He hauled himself out, panting with exhaustion, and came to her side.

'I have to wash,' she said stiffly, shedding her heavy-duty gloves. When she returned, he made no comment that she'd put on a skirt and a fresh shirt.

It was early for lunch, but the maid had laid out bowls of gazpacho and freshly baked bread, with cold tortilla and fruit. When she sat down, she discovered to her surprise that she was ravenous. Julio ate sparingly, lounging on a sunbed, still in his alarmingly minimal briefs, the dark gleaming expanse of his body making her nervous. So she ate as a diversion.

'You said you'd tell me what changes you're making

to Steve's business,' she said coldly, starting on her second hunk of bread.

'I'm expanding it.'

'Why?' she asked bluntly.

'Power.' Julio slipped on his sunglasses and stretched out on the lounger, nibbling a peach in a desultory way. 'I love it,' he murmured. The juice fell to his chest and she almost leaned over to wipe it up with her finger, but stopped herself just in time. 'And because I'm not prepared to be associated with any tatty, half-baked operations. I'll be taking on people to cope with the contract work and this garden. You're wasting your talents here.'

'Thanks,' she said sarcastically. 'At the risk of a smutty answer, where do my talents lie?' More juice flowed down his hand and on to his chest. It began to trickle down the line defining the centre of his ribs and Randall watched in fascination.

'Design and ideas.'

Randall's heart beat faster. Just what she longed for. And, as a member of the old society, he could land contracts that she and Steve had drooled over from a distance. 'Anywhere in mind?' she asked casually.

'You'll cut your teeth first and please me first before you're let loose on anyone else,' he replied.

'I don't like the idea of pleasing you,' she frowned.

He grinned mocking. 'Cast your eyes over my farm a few miles from here. I've been having it renovated. Now I want some ideas about landscaping the grounds.' A few miles. She considered that information. It would mean a longer drive to see Tom each evening. 'You have no evidence to show clients that you have talent. You'll need a showpiece, photographs, a video, a satisfied client, to show to prospective customers. Use my farm for that purpose.' Julio sat up and swung his legs to the ground, leaning forwards and putting a hand on her knee. 'Santini promised you his patronage. You have mine now.'

'I'm not sure I want it,' she said doubtfully, removing the hand as if it were something unpleasant, 'if it means working for you.'

'You don't think that's all the leverage I'm using on you, do you?' he enquired silkily. 'When I go for something, I do it *thoroughly*. I'm moving the business to another site and ordering equipment, drawing boards, machinery, vehicles. If I'm getting you to landscape gardens for the jet-set, then the operation needs to look classy.'

Randall carefully laid down her fork, her heart thudding with a mixture of excitement and apprehension. 'I have a feeling that you're about to say "but",' she said in a low tone.

'Very perceptive,' he smiled, his eyes unreadable behind the black mirrors.

She could see herself, however, leaning forward anxiously, and so she hastily sat back, dabbing at her mouth and taking a piece of manchego cheese delicately in her fingers. This was it, she thought. The end of her dreams. 'I'm not interested if you expect me to show my gratitude on the horticultural equivalent of the casting couch,' she said shortly.

'I suppose that would be a hot bed,' he said drily. 'Relax. All I want is your garden expertise,' he murmured. 'Landscaping generates high profits and I'm into money-making schemes. So I'll inject capital into the business because I think you can earn money for me. I sit back and do nothing, you work.'

'Like a pimp and his prostitute?' she suggested sourly.

Julio's mouth twitched. 'I suppose so. However, I like the idea of making money out of you legally. Let's face it, people here are bored with the same crowd of architects and designers producing the same tired ideas. You'll bring a breath of fresh air into their jaded lives. And what fun it'll be to use your talents,' he said persuasively.

'But,' she prompted warily.

'But,' he acknowledged, 'I expect you to remain here after work. I don't want you sliding off to see friends without my knowledge, or meeting men. There'll be no promiscuity. You'll stay in your cottage and not leave the land. I expect to have control over who you see and where you go.'

Randall's eyes rounded. 'I can't do that!' she gasped indignantly. 'You can't curtail my right to come and go as I please!'

He shrugged. 'I have the whip hand, Randall. I can do almost anything I like. If you want a future in this country, you'd better agree. Or...' The rest of the sentence hung in the air like the sword of Damocles over her head.

'Tell me about the ''or'',' she said resentfully.

'With pleasure. Or I'll sell all the equipment, the yard, the business. And you'd be out of a job,' he said softly with the triumph of a man who knew he'd backed his prey into a corner.

'Blackmail, Julio?' she asked coldly. Stay and be seduced, pretty maiden, your fortune awaits... Refuse and be ruined.

She drew in her breath harshly and gave him a jaundiced look. All her instincts prompted her to tell him to go to hell. If she'd been alone in the world, she would have done just that and perhaps helped him there with her fists. But she had responsibilities.

'Your honesty can be blinding, sometimes,' she said, trying to keep her voice from sounding panic-stricken. 'Be reasonable,' she begged.

'I am. You'll get a lot out of this.'

'I'm aware of that,' she replied evenly, instead of smashing plates on his head—and hating herself for the restraint but of course she had to coax Julio around. She wanted the job; it was everything she'd worked for and it was about to land in her lap. But she couldn't spend days, weeks, maybe, without seeing Tom—that was unthinkable!

Sighing, knowing she had to play ball with Julio, she decided to bore him rigid with her refusal to sleep with him and hope he'd get homesick, return to Argentina and leave her to run the business in peace. If he didn't... The hysteria rose inside her and she ruthlessly repressed it.

'I know you were annoyed because I slipped out to see my friends last night,' she said, carefully modulating her voice. 'I think you'd approve of them, though. They're a married couple with children and I visit them often. You know I like space around me; that I feel crushed and miserable if I'm contained. I need freedom; no one knows that better than you,' she said earnestly. 'Let me spend my evenings where I choose and we might have a deal going.' In agitation she put her hand on his sleeve and turned the full power of her intense blue eyes on him. 'Please,' she said huskily. 'I'm begging you.'

Thoughtfully he took her hand in his and tightened his grip. 'You want the work, then,' he said softly.

'Of course I do. You know that,' she said bitterly. 'Think how ambitious I am. Would I risk a scandal? You won't be embarrassed by any sleazy or immoral associations because of me, I promise.'

'I don't want clients thinking you stay out all night,' he frowned. 'OK. I'll compromise. Tell me when and where you go so I can contact you if I wish. Report back to me by midnight every evening. That's the only concession you're getting.'

'Perhaps,' she muttered, loathing the hold he had over her. 'I'd better mention now that I'm going to a wedding tomorrow on my day off.' A blissful smile gently lifted her mouth, transforming her unhappy face. Ana's sister was marrying an actor and Tom was to be a pageboy— in a sweet little matador's suit that made her heart somersault when she saw him in it.

'In what church?' Julio asked softly, his thumb idly rubbing backwards and forwards on her wrist.

'I don't want you there!' she said hastily.

Julio was motionless, his mouth grim. 'I don't go to weddings,' he said quietly.

'No, of course,' Randall said with gentle compassion, sensing that emotion was overwhelming him. 'I understand. I'll be at San Pedro, in Málaga.' She was safe. It was unlikely he'd personally check it out. She slipped from his grasp and wandered over to lean on the wooden fence that separated the pool terrace from a sunken rock garden.

'You're undecided about this, aren't you?' he observed.

She frowned at an inoffensive tiger-jaw plant. 'I'm not sure about your motivations.' Hearing his step, she braced herself for his touch, the inevitable physical persuasion. His arm came around her shoulders but she remained stiff and unresponsive.

'Think carefully about this. I can give you the chance to secure the present and the future for yourself and make the kind of life you choose. I'm not exactly exerting myself, Randall,' he said wryly. 'It will only take a small amount of capital to make the business thrive. What will *really* make it work is your expertise and imagination. Without that, nothing will happen at all. You'll be the one creating the income and I'll take a cut of the profit.'

'I don't know—' she said uncertainly.

'I'm acting for selfish interests as usual. That's why I'd sell the business on, if I didn't get your co-operation. That's perfectly understandable, isn't it? Why should I put money in for someone who kicks me in the teeth?'

It made sense. He was getting a lot in return for her work. 'Well…' She glared at the little cactus again. It had managed to grow and flower without much help from anyone. A smile illuminated her face. 'You put in money, I put in my skills. That sounds like a partnership. An equal partnership,' she said daringly. 'I'll agree on those terms if you don't interfere—'

He grunted. 'From thousands of miles away? Once it's set up, I know you can run something like this with the right staff.'

Although this was what Randall wanted—for Julio to leave the country and to run her own business—the corners of her mouth drooped contrarily. 'Terrific,' she said, injecting a brightness into her tone that she didn't feel.

'Shake on it,' he said huskily. She looked at the hand and then at him. Hesitantly her fingers stretched towards his and were clasped firmly then released. 'Our fates are sealed,' he smiled.

Then he dropped a kiss on her cheek, patted her bottom as though she'd behaved like a good little girl, just as he'd planned, and sauntered off before she had a chance to pat his bottom in return. They were partners, after all.

But despite her victory, Randall had the distinct sensation that Julio had got exactly what he'd wanted and that she was still dancing to his tune. Even if she couldn't think of any snags at all, not for the life of her.

As she had expected, it was a wonderful wedding and Tom looked adorable. Knowing that Julio was unlikely to make an appearance meant Randall could relax and enjoy herself, the deluge of compliments about her new outfit making her flushed and excited.

It was certainly a cracker. Blue to match her eyes, a softly swirling mid-thigh taffeta skirt, a wide belt around her small waist, bootlace-strap chemise top in a deeper blue silk and a perfectly tailored jacket. Her hat was a nonsense of a pillbox sitting on her carefully upswept hair while a gardenia tucked in the darker blue veil gave her huge eyes a mysterious look.

She always enjoyed family occasions in Spain. It was amazing how much children were loved, how they were passed from one person to another to be admired and exclaimed over. It must, she thought, have been like this for Julio. No wonder he'd hated his first week at school, deprived of all that attention.

Standing dreamily by a window, she let a rush of images engulf her, seeing—instead of the wedding guests—the figure of Julio in the walled garden of Broadfield on his second day of term. He was stripping off his jacket and cap with a demonic fury and she'd watched in awe while he threw the garments on to the bonfire and watched them burn with an exciting savagery.

Their eyes had met across the flames, their faces lit by an unholy light and, in the way of tomboyish ten-year-old girls, she had thrown a clod of earth at him to establish their friendship. Randall smiled gently, remembering how he'd chased her around the garden and finally fallen headlong with her into the swimming-pool. Fire and water. Two violent baptisms of the heart.

Overwhelmed with the poignant emotions, Randall sought her son and swept him into her arms. 'Dance with me,' she said with a laugh, hiding her wistfulness. 'Let's do a crazy dance!'

She drove back just after eleven, merrily singing a duet with Placido Domingo and discovered that Julio was having a party. The headlights of her truck fell on dozens of cars parked far up the road—luxury-market cars, mostly ostentatious, with one or two stretch limos propping up bored chauffeurs.

A slight excess of champagne and happiness made her giggle at a mischievous idea that had come into her mind. Instead of quietly reporting back to Julio, she'd do it in style now she was his partner!

With great dignity, she drove right in the front gate, earning herself a chorus of wolf whistles and the usual predictable remarks as her rusty old truck rattled and jolted past the limos and rolled to a stop, a Mercedes

touching her front bumper and a gleaming Ferrari on either side. Three chauffeurs helped her down and laugh-
ingly pointed her towards a small group of tuxedo-clad
guests who stared in astonishment from the open doorway.

With enormous aplomb, Randall checked her hat was
still tilted at the right angle, smoothed down her skirt and
stalked majestically to the brightly lit house.

'*Hello*, gorgeous!' drawled a man in the hall with a fat
cigar twiddling in his hand. His accent marked him out
as an ex-cockney and made her feel instantly at home.
'Am I lookin' at the classy cabaret number or am I
dreamin'?'

'I could manage a chorus of "Any Old Iron", if you
like,' she smiled. 'But nothing more demanding. The
Marquis and I are business partners. Excuse me.'

'Goofed again! Pardon me for askin',' apologised Fat
Cigar hastily. 'Tell you what, I'll shove a way through
the crowd. The Marquis's got a million women hanging
on his braces. One's my wife, the other's my ex.' Randall
laughed, liking the man at once, and strolled through the
sea of faces feeling rather like a celebrity. 'Gawd! He's
up to his nostrils in perfume and bath oil, poor soul. See
what I mean?' the man murmured.

She saw. Julio's raven head topped all others in the
room and particularly those of the women around him.
Despite his apparent rapt attention on a tangle-haired redhead who was tapping his broken nose playfully, his
glance flew to Randall as if he knew instinctively that she
had arrived.

The noise around her dimmed, the party ceased to exist
in that look, slow, lingering, evoking a warm glow inside
her that spread from her toes to her tingling scalp. 'I'm
back,' she mouthed superfluously and he nodded, delighting her with the open admiration in his eyes. His view
was from her chin upwards; what might he think of the

rest of her? A shiver of delicious anticipation ran through her body. It was going to be a waste, taking off her finery without Julio seeing it. Slinky fish-tail outfit it wasn't, but she did look good.

'Sure you said…business partner?' asked a voice in her ear.

She grinned wryly at Fat Cigar's very reasonable doubt. 'He made a takeover bid for the company I work for, and promoted me.'

'Wise man.'

'Wise, perhaps, but he's burdened with a load of Spanish machismo,' she said wryly. 'I'm checking in. And out again.'

'You've only just arrived! Go on, make all the men here drool down their shirt-fronts. Drive my wives mad with jealousy and dance with me,' suggested her escort.

'I don't…' Randall shot a glance at Julio. He was still watching her and the redhead was drifting a hand around his neck, drawing it down towards a pair of scarlet-slashed lips. She grinned mischievously. 'I'd love to dance,' she said impulsively. 'To be honest,' she said, suddenly deciding to enjoy herself, 'I feel I could party all night.'

'Stun me!' The cigar was hastily abandoned on a drinks tray and she was being led outside to the softly lit terrace where a small band played smoochy music.

Julio detached himself from the redhead as she slipped a piece of paper in his pocket. Probably her phone number, thought Randall. She knew, with a thrill of expectation, that he was heading towards her. Clasped to her partner's chest, she caught occasional glimpses of Julio forging his way through the guests, pausing to reply to them with brief, courteous remarks and side-stepping the women who bore down on him. Tension gripped her as she mentally counted how many steps he needed to take to reach her…

'So naturally we all dumped our previous engagements,' her partner was saying, 'and accepted like a shot. The wife's always fancied a gander at this place, same as everyone here. No one from the Spanish aristocracy's asked us to a party before—and the rumours about your mate the Marquis would make your hair curl.'

'Oh?' Randall detached herself from the white shirt-front with a gentle push of her hand and looked at him with interest. 'All these people are strangers to the Marquis?'

'Yeah. Some maid of his got chauffeured around, delivering the invites. He chose his area, mind. Millionaires' Row, they call it down our way. Short of cash, is he?' he asked shrewdly.

Randall's laugh tinkled out. 'No! He's chucking it around! What are these rumours about our mysterious Marquis?' she asked, fascinated. 'Come on,' she coaxed, when he hesitated.

'Dunno. Some scandal. I'd get arrested if I told you half the theories why he never came back to claim his lands.'

'His mother was Argentinian,' explained Randall. 'He'd lived there all his life.'

'Yeah, but this is his roots, his Dad's place, and his sister lives here. They're close, these aristos. Someone sneezes, they fly in with flowers. Your partner's never shown his face here or at any of the usual shindigs that haul them haughty Spaniards in from all over the globe, not even the Feria and that's like missing your own birthday. He's got some woman out there who's got her hooks in him. That's what keeps him out of circulation. But ask around and mouths close as tight as a fist in a punch-up.'

'I'm not sure he's interested in social events,' she began, defending Julio. 'Perhaps—' She paused, knowing by instinct that Julio was behind her before he even spoke.

'Perhaps,' he said suavely, 'you would forgive me if I spoke for a few minutes to Miss Slade?'

'We was talkin' about you,' said Fat Cigar, not in the least embarrassed.

'I know,' murmured Julio, absently emptying his pockets of a handful of scraps of paper, all with hastily scribbled phone numbers. She wondered if he was letting her know how devastatingly attractive he was to other women. 'May I prise your partner away?' he persisted smoothly.

'I knew she was on loan,' sighed Fat Cigar. 'My mum warned me that Paradise never lasts.'

'I'm optimistic that it does,' murmured Julio, taking Randall in his arms.

'I'll see you again, I hope,' she smiled at Fat Cigar.

'Sure,' he grinned. 'We'll have that sing-song. A good old knees-up at the piano with the missus. OK?'

'I'll practise,' she answered warmly. Her hands automatically slid to Julio's shoulders and they glided away. Oddly enough, she felt immediately content. They stood swaying to the music and she found herself smiling for the duration of one dance and then the next.

'I think we'd better move,' whispered Julio finally. 'Though I'm not sure I can.'

Disturbed from her reverie, Randall blinked. 'I only came to say I'd returned—' Her breath jerked out as her body was pressed against his black watered silk waistcoat and she felt the warmth of his cheek against hers. He wore a gardenia like hers in his buttonhole and the crush of their bodies released its heady fragrance into the air. They both inhaled at the same time and then smiled because of their shared reaction.

Julio's hands were moving on the soft silk of her jacket, enjoying how it curved sensuously into the dip of her back. There was a rustle as his fingers moved over her taffeta-clad hips. Then his fingertips had strayed to the top of her thigh. At first she wished she'd worn a longer skirt and then she had to admit she was lying to herself.

'You are quite impossibly beautiful,' he said softly, smiling into her eyes. 'Very, very dishy.'

'Makes a change from juggling-bear T-shirts, I suppose,' she said nervously.

'It has the same effect,' he murmured. 'I want to touch you so badly, in sinfully tempting places, that I'm seriously thinking of shouting "Fire!" and clearing the whole damn place. Then,' he said speculatively, 'I'd lie through my teeth and persuade you that my shower is the only safe place to be.'

Fire and water, she thought shakily and then her eyes widened as he moved his body against hers to alert her to his need. 'Julio! For shame! I won't be ravished on a dance-floor!' she protested. 'Have some respect for your partner.'

'I have, or you'd be on the floor by now,' he drawled. 'You know,' he mused softly, bending his mouth to her sensitive ear, 'I had an extraordinary sensation when you walked in. Everyone disappeared for a moment.' His solemn chocolate velvet eyes looked puzzled. 'They simply vanished and all I could see was you! Why would that be, I wonder?'

Startled by the inexplicable similarity of her sensations, Randall controlled the trembling of her fingers on the oyster satin tuxedo and she stared fixedly at the fuchsia bow-tie. 'Maybe they ran for cover because I had too much garlic at the wedding.'

'Could be.' Suddenly he kissed her, his lips gently moving on hers, coaxing them apart. 'Please,' he murmured. 'A little way. Just a fraction...' Skilfully imprisoned, she couldn't move or protest and he seemed quite oblivious to the people around them. 'Not a trace of garlic. Only the usual seductive sweetness,' he said huskily, his mouth soft from the kiss.

'Compost. In my fingernails,' she suggested weakly.

Julio took her fingers and sucked each one while

Randall's stomach twisted in delighted knots. 'No compost.' She felt the gardenia being gently removed from her veil and tucked between her breasts, Julio's thumb firm and warm and remaining in her cleavage just a fraction too long for the good of her wildly beating heart. 'You're the only woman I've ever met who dresses sensually,' he whispered. 'Textures, perfume, sound—' His hand ruffled her skirt, making it rustle.

'It's my very best outfit,' she said, trying to be safely banal. 'Cost a bomb. The wedding was lovely—and Tom…' The near-betrayal made her stumble. 'Sorry! Clumsy!' she laughed nervously, her face bright pink.

'Tom?' he enquired grimly, tensing his grip.

Somehow she recovered a few scraps of her composure. 'The—the groom…' She paused, indicating that the groom was called Tom. 'He'd brought all his actor friends, who wore the most *theatrical* clothes…'

She babbled on, aware that Julio was only half listening. He seemed content to let his hands subtly explore her, to identify where her satin briefs began and ended, to find the indent between each rib, the shape of each bone in her spinal column. It was a good thing everyone was dancing shoulder to shoulder, she thought in distraction, wriggling and protesting to no avail. Or Julio would be arrested.

'Randall,' he said reluctantly, 'I'd better let you get acquainted with a few people. I've invited—'

'Millionaires' Row,' she said with a relieved grin. 'Mr Fat Cigar told me.'

'Then start with him,' suggested Julio. 'He's obviously a fan of yours. He can be your second client when you've finished landscaping the *cortijo*—my farm.'

'Second client? Do you mean you've invited all these people for me to tout for business?' she asked in surprise.

'Why not? I knew they couldn't resist an invitation from a grandee. I imagined you'd be wearing some knock-out outfit for the wedding and it seemed a shame to waste the opportunity.'

'My goodness!' she said faintly, worrying a little that his explanation sounded a little too glib. What was he up to? 'You don't let the grass grow under your feet!'

'I've always been known for action.' His eyes mocked her wary glance. 'Never let your capital hang around doing nothing,' he explained and dropped a kiss on her nose. 'Now this is only an initial, soft approach,' he warned huskily.

'Soft approach,' she repeated, her eyes enormous and clouding with suspicion.

'Mmm. The hard sell comes later.' Julio smiled at her disarmingly. 'You know the way the game's played. Coax your target into lowering all defences, convince said target that you're harmless and decent, then slide in somewhere unexpected and make a pincer movement so that the target is surrounded, back up against the wall, deprived of supplies for some time and eventually surrenders, glad to take anything you offer.'

'It's all worked out in your mind, isn't it?' she said slowly. 'It sounds like a description of a medieval siege.' It was obviously his tried and tested strategy—whether for business or seduction, she wasn't sure.

'How else do I gain access to the ivory tower?' he said innocently.

Randall frowned. Innocence and Julio sat at opposite poles of the earth. 'I don't equate Mr Fat Cigar and his friends with living in ivory towers.'

'Sure they do, like most of us. We build our lives on half-truths and fool ourselves they're true.'

'Don't count me in on this fantasy world,' she said in warning. 'I'm not letting any wolf in shining armour climb up my hair.'

'I'm a bit muddled by the images you've painted,' Julio

grinned, 'but I get the picture. Your tower is impregnable.'

'I think only princesses live in towers,' she said sweetly. 'I'm in the yard, with the dogs.'

'Easier to get at, yards,' he drawled. She thumped his chest playfully, but felt resentfully that Julio was deliberately keeping her on edge. 'Go and talk to Mr Cigar. Chat, circulate, offer lunch to anyone promising, learn about their likes, dislikes—'

'I've done the course,' she stated, still suspicious. 'Why have you gone to all the trouble of a party for me?'

'For me,' he corrected. 'Here is the new money wandering about on two legs and dressed to kill, eager to hand its ill-gotten gains over to me. Get some design requests going and I'll move you on to the *alto sociedad* and we'll both reap the rewards. See you later. Dazzle them all.'

Although she still had doubts about his ulterior motives, Randall felt a stir of excitement in her veins. Apparently he wanted her to cut her designer's teeth on the huge new villas first, and then tackle the old society clients, with their gorgeous old properties and mature gardens. At a quick estimation, she'd have enough work for the next two hundred years.

Happily she set off to do a bit of dazzling and found that she enjoyed meeting everyone and talking to them so much that she hardly realised she was working. One group of wealthy Spaniards fell into gales of laughter at her explanation of how she'd arrived complete with battered tipper truck and parked it next to the limos. The women might be designer-dressed, the men intimidatingly elegant in hand-stitched, wide-shouldered jackets that shouted 'designer' but she felt totally at ease with them all and happily joined in the general chatter as though she'd known them all her life, especially the glamorous Consuelo.

'Come to lunch,' said Consuelo impulsively, rummaging in the chaos of her Carvela handbag for a card. 'What a mess!' she marvelled and turned to Randall with a laugh. 'My husband says I might as well live on a rubbish tip! Don't breathe a word, but sometimes I think he's right!'

'I doubt he'd like you any other way,' remarked Randall, amused. 'They say untidy women are more generous—'

'Let's not be coy. You mean better in bed!' whispered Consuelo.

Randall laughed and found Julio nudging her elbow. 'You're not dragging me away!' she protested.

'If I may.' He gave a courteous dip of his head.

'Next Wednesday? Midday. The address is there,' said Consuelo, her smooth hand on Randall's arm. 'We'll talk about untidy women, eh?'

'I'd love that,' giggled Randall. 'I'll look forward to it.'

Julio bowed again and moved her away. 'I thought you'd like to see the Gitanos,' he murmured. 'I bribed a group to come from the caves in Sacromonte. Don't worry, it all goes down on expenses. Incidentally,' he said casually, an arm around her waist as he guided her outside, 'I'm glad you found it so easy to get on with the aristos.'

'The what?'

Julio laughed and pulled her to a chair. 'My society friends,' he chuckled. 'Consuelo's a countess. The rest are either titled or descended from medieval courtiers.' Randall's mouth fell open. Gently he pushed beneath her chin to close it, grinning at her stunned expression. 'They're almost like ordinary people, aren't they?' he added innocently.

'Ha very ha,' she glowered, but added a rueful smile because she didn't resent his deception. If she'd known, she would never have approached them. As it was, she'd established a friendly rapport and received a welcome she would never have expected. Plus several invitations to family lunch—a rare honour—in addition to Consuelo's date with her. Ordinary people…yes, they were, really.

'Forgive me?' Julio slanted his eyes at her. 'I thought you should bear it in mind that in old Spain you can be at home with anyone, rich or poor, jet-setter or shop assistant. Whatever you think to the contrary, we don't know the meaning of class. Perhaps on the Costa there are demarcations. Not so here.'

Randall felt enormously pleased that she'd found it so easy to mix and her self-esteem had gone up several notches as a result. 'I thought you were very class-conscious,' she said quietly. 'The matrons seemed to think so at Broadfield.'

He stilled. 'Tell me,' he murmured softly.

'Oh, it began one Open Day,' she sighed. 'You'd been rather reserved for a while and I was worried that you were bored with me. And then the school was filled with smart people in incredible clothes who talked in china-clear accents about opera and social events and it suddenly dawned on me with a blinding clarity that I was only the gardener's daughter and you were the son of a blue-blooded aristocrat.'

'Had I ever said that I gave a damn about your background?' he said with a frown.

'No, but that's when the matrons put me wise.' For the first time, Randall discovered that she could talk about it and not feel hurt.

'They were jealous of you,' observed Julio shrewdly.

'I know,' she said without rancour. 'They were all in love with you.'

'I meant that you were gorgeous and they weren't,' he corrected drily.

She giggled at the preposterous idea. 'I know what I was, and it wasn't gorgeous! The matrons made that plain.

They showed me the boys' mothers and sisters who were idolising you on the terrace below and then they shoved me in front of a mirror. I saw myself as a different kind of person for the first time. My knees were grubby, my legs were covered in scratches from clearing brambles and my hands were stained with blackberry juice!'

Julio chuckled. 'And yet…that same night at the dance you turned up looking the most wanton, desirable woman I'd ever seen,' he said, his voice thickening with desire.

'You remember?' she asked shakily.

'How could I forget?' he husked. Randall's heart lurched. But she'd never know if he meant that, or was handing her a line, she thought wistfully. 'So they taunted you, trying to make you feel worthless,' he frowned. 'Was that why you deliberately drove me crazy that night?'

Randall lowered her head and took an intense interest in her feet for a while to hide her blushes. ''Fraid so,' she admitted. 'I wanted to prove the matrons wrong. Dad taught me to fight when I'm attacked. And I needed to convince myself that you cared for me a little,' she mumbled. 'It was a matter of pride.'

'And unnecessary,' he sighed. 'Don't you know even now, why I'd been trying to keep away from you?'

'No,' she answered warily.

'Because I wanted to rip all your clothes off, every time I saw you,' he said baldly, and blushes scalded her face and sped hotly through her body. He chuckled huskily, causing a sexual shiver to chase the blushes. 'I was desperate for sex, but I didn't want to upset or frighten you. The classic dilemma.'

'I shouldn't have acted the vamp,' she mumbled.

'It's true to say,' he drawled in amusement, 'that you put paid to any vestiges of control I might have had when you walked in wearing that incredible white cotton dress—'

'It was awfully cheap—'

'Who noticed?' he purred, lightly stroking her arm.
'Every inch of you was issuing a sexual challenge. The
whole temperature in the room went up ten degrees, the
masters were apoplectic. God knows how my friends kept
their hands off you.'

He hadn't, of course, she thought, her throat closing up.
They'd made love that night: wild, uninhibited love. Or
rather, lust. Was that what he was seeking now? Sexual
comfort? Isabel was in Argentina; she was here. Julio was
so virile. Her body trembled uncontrollably. He was hungry. She'd given in once. Why not again, he must be
thinking?

And so was she. Why not again? Every inch of her skin
was aware of him, every nerve, every fibre of her being.
And with the click of castanets, as a lone dark-eyed gypsy
on the terrace began to lift his arms in a graceful arc and
stamp his feet, she felt her mind saying to the rhythm,
Why not, why not, *why not*?

CHAPTER EIGHT

THE chatter from the guests became an expectant hush. She and Julio sat side by side, thigh to thigh beneath the warm night sky. The music of a *zambra* filled her body with fire, the movements of the proud male gypsy both restrained and passionate. Like Julio: the two opposite sides of Spanish character, ever fighting for domination.

A black-eyed woman lifted slender arms and slowly clicked her castanets, ruffling her flounced skirt to attract the haughty male dancer's attention. The courtship began, slow, seductive and tantalising, both dancers holding themselves in check as they executed the strictly disciplined steps—and yet managing to indicate the promise of a fire that would flare into life, given the slightest encouragement.

Beside her she knew that Julio's senses were igniting. His hand grasped hers more tightly, his body pressed more urgently. Randall knew she had to get away, before the music and Julio made her forget caution entirely and he broke her defences.

'I think I should go. It's late,' she whispered.

'Falling under the gypsy spell?' he murmured softly, stroking her bare thigh. 'You must stay. Or insult them.'

Her chair was in too prominent a position for a discreet exit, she realised. With reluctant resignation she tried to block out the sound but wasn't very successful because the beat had become part of her body, vibrating the very ground.

Julio's thumb rubbed up and down in a maddening rhythm in time with the music. Heavy pulses throbbed with compelling urgency inside her. In a vain attempt to divert the alarming focus of her mind and body, she wriggled on the seat. Julio's thumb paused. She shot him a look.

He was making love to her again, she thought weakly. Battering her with sensual feelings. The only sure way to reach her. She gazed warily into his dark eyes and felt the repressed tension in his body increase. Her lashes fluttered down to where his stilled hand lay on her thigh and she bit her lip.

I want him, she moaned inside, her head slowly tipping back in shame at her need, and a wash of heat made her skin prickle so fiercely that she craved the cool night air on her body. Almost without thinking, she slipped off her jacket and heard Julio's harsh intake of breath. He stared hungrily at her lifting breasts and a sharply spearing excitement spread from each tight centre till her whole nervous system was clamouring for his touch, while the crushed petals of the gardenia filled her nostrils with dizzying perfume.

She saw his fingers go to his mouth and then bring them, slicked wet with his tongue, to the back of her knee. Even anticipating it couldn't prevent her pelvis from jerking. The faint movement on her smooth, sensitive skin made her head spin, her eyes drowsy, her lips softly part.

Sound filled the air, husky, triumphant, encouraging. She could hardly separate Julio's hypnotic seduction of her from the whirling figures on the stage as they stamped and strutted in a compellingly controlled frenzy, sensuous, pliant, intensely provocative. Their movements became faster and faster till they forgot the watching audience, lost in their own needs, sweat pouring from their bodies and slicking their black hair as they let loose all their pent-up passion in a wild, shockingly sexual frenzy that ended in a shattering climax.

After the final guttural cries had died away there was a stunned silence before everyone rose to their feet in a standing ovation. Only Julio's arms, helping her up, made it possible for Randall to stand.

'Are you all right?' he asked hoarsely.

Not trusting her voice, she nodded and concentrated on clapping the exhausted dancers, feeling as if she'd come out of a trance, like them. And when Julio gently excused himself and went up to thank the Gitanos, she fled, managing to smile and nod her way through the still-applauding guests on the lawn till she reached the dark path to her cottage and, at last, was safe inside and alone, wishing she had Tom there to cuddle, to love.

Sliding off her rustling taffeta skirt, she stepped out of it and then raised her arms to remove the silky top, catching her breath as it slithered over her body like a lover's touch. In her fevered imagination, she wondered what it would be like to spend the night with Julio, a whole night of exquisitely drawn-out torment and delight.

Her face flamed at her thoughts. But when she hung her clothes in the cupboard she found that she was doing so quietly, so that she could hear the slightest sound outside. Half naked, she stood in shocked dismay. It was Julio she was listening for, hoping he'd come—even though she knew she could never allow him to relieve the unbearable demands of her body.

So why hope? Why start at every sound outside? Her mind seemed torn in two. She was two people: a mother and a deeply moral woman...a quickly aroused hussy, with a shameful sexual appetite.

'Idiot,' she muttered, trying to find the straight and narrow again. But she hadn't only lost the path, she thought wryly, she'd almost found herself in bed with the wolf!

The feeling of disappointment when he didn't come was overwhelming. She heard the cars driving away, the sound of laughter and people calling their goodbyes to each other. In tense expectation, she waited and listened till it was clear that Julio had decided to leave her alone.

This was his way, she thought. He was winding her up

till she snapped. Already her body leapt into life at a mere glance of his smouldering eyes—and this was only the soft sell. When he really began to exert all his masculine persuasion, she'd find herself in a lot of trouble.

Politely, sitting beneath the shade of the chestnut tree the next morning, they exchanged information about the people they'd met at the party. Nothing was said about her abrupt departure. Randall wryly decided that this was part of his strategy. Attack, confuse, disappear. Sounded like an SAS operation, she thought glumly, wishing she'd had the life-renewing fun of breakfast with Tom to help her face the day.

'Concentrate, Randall,' drawled Julio lazily.

'I am,' she answered, conjuring up a blithe smile.

'I mean, on the list,' he said sardonically.

She thinned her mouth. 'I *am*,' she lied, and he laughed, not deceived at all.

By the time Julio had checked her contacts at the party with the list of guests and discussed those to approach first, it was almost eleven. And she was appalled to discover that she was being driven mad by his casual businesslike manner that barely acknowledged her as a woman.

This, she frowned, was even despite the fact that she wore a feminine skirt and top in a buttery silk faille. She groaned inwardly, realising how contrary her behaviour had become. Any moment now, she thought, disgusted with herself, she'd sigh and wriggle and start blinding him with female tricks like fluttering eyelashes and wide-eye glances.

'You're pouting.' His lips enclosed hers before she had time to blink. 'I think it's time we went,' he murmured, laughter in his voice.

'Went where?' she asked breathlessly, wishing her reflexes weren't so slow. Or so fast. She'd returned the kiss for a split second.

'To the farm,' he answered, gathering up all the papers. 'Cook's done us a picnic and some supplies. The sooner you get the visit done and the garden designed, the quicker you can start on the stuff that'll earn us money.'

'I don't like the sound of that. You mean I'm doing work for you without being paid?' she complained. 'I need money, Julio.' She clammed up in case he thought he could buy her. Julio smiled in a worryingly meaningful way and said no more.

They cruised panther-like in the low black car, deep into the fertile countryside, snaking up into the mountains on a narrow road. Limestone crags jutted against the hard blue sky and waterfalls thundered into ravines, feeding the complex drainage systems in the olive groves. An occasional finger-winged eagle soared on the thermals, flying free.

Free. That's how I'm feeling, Randall thought suddenly, and she took a deep breath of the perfumed air, slipping off her shoes and wriggling her toes in contentment. 'I've never been this far inland,' she confided casually, leaning out of the window to follow the bright yellow flash of a woodpecker flying over a field of dazzling white cistus. She drew her head in again and pushed the golden strands of her hair vaguely into place. 'It's been such hard work, dashing up and down the Costa on the contract work. I've never even been to Granada. I'd love to see the gardens there,' she added wistfully.

'You must go. The gardens of the Generalife and the Alhambra Palace are unmissable. It's not surprising the Moors wanted to stay,' Julio said casually. 'The snows on the Sierra Nevada and the constant supply of water must have transfixed them with delight after the desert landscapes. My farm, the Cortijo Arabe, is almost as old as the Alhambra,' he offered surprisingly.

'Built by the Arabs?' she asked eagerly. Julio nodded, an absent, affectionate expression on his face. He loves the farm, she thought and wondered why it had become abandoned, why he had remained in Argentina if he felt that strongly. 'Tell me about it,' she said curiously.

'It was built in the thirteenth century for an Arabian noble. When they were driven out of Spain it was modernised.' He flashed her an amused grin. 'That would be in the late fifteenth century. It stayed generally untouched until my father gave it a face-lift and it later became neglected and run-down—'

'Why?' she asked quietly, suddenly alert.

'Lovely though it is,' he said softly, his caressing voice confirming his feelings for the farm, 'my mother pined for Argentina. Father loved her so much that he gave up Andalucía to live where she would be happy.'

'Like…you did for Elvira,' she muttered to herself.

Julio's thick lashes swept downwards. 'Please,' he said harshly. 'I told you I didn't want to think of her.'

Randall gave him an apologetic look. 'Sorry. And…I was sad to read in the newspapers that your parents had died,' she said awkwardly. 'I thought of you then.' It occurred to her that she'd been an avid reader of the foreign news, greedy for information about Julio. He'd never really left her heart at all. She watched the black-shadowed ravines pass by and the silver sparkle of the violently tumbling rivers. 'I'd hate to leave here,' she sighed. 'I suppose you feel the same way about Argentina now.'

'We—I'm…settled on the ranch.'

He began to chatter about the plants in his garden there but she turned her attention off, her mind fixed on that one word: 'we'. It was quite obvious that he was attempting to divert her attention from his slip-up, but she was determined to hold it in her head and not forget it. Whenever she found herself weakening in Julio's arms, she'd bring it to mind.

We. Julio and Isabel. The woman he loved.

Steeling her soul, she pulled herself together. 'Can you give me a quick run-down on what needs doing on the farm?' she said coolly, interrupting a long discourse on black bulls.

'Yes, if you like. Uh…the cypress avenue is nearing the end of its life. That must be underplanted. I think we need a shelter belt to the east. We're just coming up to the entrance and… Damn! Where did they come from?'

He drew the car to a halt at the top of a cypress avenue stretching into the distance and jumped out to shoo a herd of goats from a small orchard of peaches and apricots.

'Come and help!' he called urgently, over the melodious clanging of goat-bells.

Randall leapt out to join him, racing around in an attempt to drive the agile goats through a gap in a fence on the far side of the orchard. 'They'll be back the minute we go,' she warned.

'I know,' he frowned. 'They've been eating the new shoots. Santini only planted the trees last winter.'

She studied the tubes of wire mesh that surrounded each tree. The goats had pushed in the netting to reach the tender shoots. 'We can weave some branches in the netting and make a barrier,' she suggested.

'That's a good idea,' he said admiringly.

She was in her element. 'The branches will keep the goats off till I can make a proper guard for each tree. I'll get some gorse branches. You strip some fan palms for me to tie them in place.'

'Like the old days, isn't it?' he said throatily. 'Working together—'

'It's not like the old days *at all*,' she said curtly and walked off to tear branches from the gorse bushes with unusual violence.

'Afraid of being with me?' he queried, unfairly close to her ear.

She whirled on him angrily. 'No! Annoyed! You think you only have to smile and be charming and press a few buttons and I'll be jelly at your feet. You think that having a few gypsies dance will make me swoon. You'd better wise up, Julio. It takes more than that to touch inside me where it really matters. You might think I'm a slut because I welcomed your lovemaking when we were eighteen. But I gave you everything I had because I loved you and for no other reason. Whereas now, I don't trust you and I'd never let a man I don't trust make love to me.'

'So you deny your instincts,' he growled.

'They let me down before,' she pointed out bitterly. 'And something in my mind died when you ditched me. Something in my heart got taken away. Getting involved with you in any relationship other than a business one would be suicide. So please don't make a pass. Don't expect to make love to me. And please don't tell me this is like old times. You were single and unattached then, I was innocent. We've changed more than you know.'

'But I'm unattached again,' he husked, drawing her resisting body to his.

Cold and rigid, she met his drowsy eyes with her steady gaze. 'Liar! I think you're forgetting Isabel,' she said in glacial tones.

Julio froze. He let her go abruptly, his face paling. 'What do you know about her?' he growled.

'Everything,' she replied, elaborating wildly.

'*Maldito*… Who told you?' he demanded sharply. 'Santini? Someone at the party?'

So the woman was generally known as his official mistress. Randall's stomach flipped with jealousy. 'It doesn't matter,' she said wearily. 'You love her, don't you?'

He nodded. 'Yes, but…Randall, what I feel for her— Are you crying?' he husked, his finger reaching out to slick up a huge, salty tear.

'No!' she said shakily.

Julio's mouth quirked up at one corner. 'Jealous of Isabel?' he enquired, suddenly alert.

'Don't be ridiculous!' she snapped. 'It's probably hay fever.'

'Are you sure you know who she is?' His voice came in a knee-weakening caress.

'Even with my limited education I can work that one out,' she said haughtily. 'You'd only been married a month when Elvira died so she's not your child. Your mother is dead and you have no more immediate family, so that leaves only one relationship I can think of that would make you whisper sweet nothings on the phone.'

She'd said that quite calmly, she thought in relief, warily studying Julio's solemn face to see if he believed that she was indifferent to the state of his heart.

'Well, you seem to have got it sussed out,' he acknowledged.

'We know where we stand, don't we?' she said coldly.

He chuckled. 'I think we do, Randall.'

That was something to be glad about. She hated him. But it made things easier. Now he'd admitted his feelings for Isabel, he couldn't pretend to woo her with lies and protestations of love. It was unlikely he'd attempt to touch her again.

She gritted her teeth to stem the misery. It felt as if he'd betrayed her for the second time. And while they silently built the barriers around the tender fruit trees, she was building her own barriers, erecting pricklier defences, stiffening her resolve. And desperately fighting the tears.

The orchard gave way to a stand of ancient cork oaks, the naked wood a dark blood-red where their bark had been stripped and harvested. Beyond a hump-backed bridge spanning an idling river, sprawled the farm. Its whitewashed walls sat beneath oriental domes and tiled Spanish towers in a surprisingly harmonious blend of styles that won Randall's admiration immediately.

'Storks are nesting on the tower,' Julio pointed out. 'It means good luck.'

'I need it,' she said grimly, and decided there and then that any luck flying around would be grabbed by her. She and Tom needed it most.

'Can't we share it, since we're partners?' he asked with faint amusement.

'We share a business. That's all. I hope you'll keep that in mind.' She slid out of the car before he came to help her because she didn't want to be touched. 'I like the palm trees,' she said, deliberately detached.

Inhaling the champagne air, she surveyed the semicircular terrace and the incomparable view over a sea of olive trees and umbrella pines in the valleys below. And her cool hauteur vanished in an instant.

'It's lovely,' she breathed, weakening. Where the land had been tilled, the soil glowed cinnamon-red, but elsewhere the fields rippled in the breeze with wave upon wave of colour: violet, purple, saffron and rose; clover, clary, buttercup and cranesbill. 'Beautiful,' she sighed.

'Go on in,' said Julio huskily, touching her shoulder. He withdrew his hand abruptly when she lifted her entranced face to his. 'Look around, enjoy. I'll bring in the picnic.'

With the smoothness belying its centuries-old hinges, the cedarwood door swung open, throwing shafts of sunlight into an echoing, shuttered hall. Feeling a sense of excitement, Randall raised the latches in the shutters and flung them wide, revealing their exquisite flower paintings to the bright light of day.

'Good grief!' she exclaimed, seeing the large hamper Julio was bringing in. 'You've brought enough food for six people!'

'Oh, do you think so?' Julio asked casually. 'I told Cook you had a huge appetite, and she loves to feed me up. I'll put this in the cool room. Be with you in a moment.'

Happily wandering from room to room, her mind filled with impressions of richly polished furniture, intricate plasterwork ceilings and Persian wall tiles, Randall entered one that took her breath away. It lay open to the sky and the wheeling, screaming swallows, and focused on an ornate stone fountain.

Pausing by the arched doorway, she reached out to fondle the rustling taffeta drapes. They were the same forest-green as the leaf design on the floor tiles. On an impulse, she put her cheek to the material and then stiffened when she felt Julio's hand on her back.

'Silk-lined,' he said quietly, his free hand exposing the curtain lining. 'Feel.' He drew the soft fabric across her face and then, as her heartbeat was quickening, he moved away. 'I chose the new furnishings. Fabric was flying regularly between here and the ranch. They've hung them well. I hope you like them.'

'You always did have a good eye for texture and colour,' she replied a little shakily.

'I flatter myself that I have a good eye for beauty, too,' he said softly, his dark eyes lingering on her.

From a fog-bound brain, Randall managed to extract a coherent sentence. 'What were you going to do with the house, if you weren't intending to live here?' she asked in an oddly throaty voice.

He shrugged, his eyes veiled. 'This is part of the Quadra heritage and I must maintain it. Eventually someone in the family would have inherited the house and estates. We used to come here when we were children, but after a while it pained Father too much. I've inherited his tendency to slam doors on things that might make me vulnerable,' he mused.

Like not talking about Elvira, she thought, despite moving into another relationship with Isabel. 'The house is crying out for someone to live in it,' she said thoughtfully.

'That's the conclusion I'd come to,' he said quietly. Disconcerted, she surreptitiously watched him gazing around and she could sense a deep joy welling in him. He did love it, she thought sentimentally; it touched his heart, despite his claim to be happily settled in Argentina. Julio had a remarkable capacity to obliterate pain. 'God, it's beautiful. I'd forgotten how peaceful it could be,' he breathed. 'Tranquil, silent, serene.'

His hand rested on a fluted column, one of a forest of alabaster that formed graceful arches. The sun deepened the rich sheen of Julio's skin and Randall thought that he'd never looked more handsome than he did now, in quiet repose, lovingly contemplating the painstaking renovations that he'd masterminded with such love and care.

Randall cleared her throat and said the first thing that came into her head. 'Water channels would be wonderful here, all along the edge of the walkway. That would bring the sound of running water into the house.' Trembling under his intense gaze, she sought for inspiration and suddenly saw what was needed. 'Climbers with white or blue flowers scrambling up the thicker columns, perhaps a jacaranda tree,' she said, her growing enthusiasm making her eyes bright and excited. 'In the corner opposite that magnolia to bring out the mauves and blues in the tiles.'

'Yes,' he agreed. His molten black eyes warmed hers. 'And through here?' He reached out for her hand and, defenceless against his winning smile, she let her cool fingers be clasped by his. 'We're coming to the courtyard that forms the heart of the house,' he explained as they walked along a tiled corridor. 'My family used to spend much of their time here.'

'Oh!' she cried softly. 'I would too, if I lived in this house.' Eagerly she pulled Julio from the cloistered walk and into the tropical garden. 'Banksia roses!' she exclaimed happily, detecting their delicate fragrance.

'Listen,' said Julio, bending his head close to hers. 'What do you hear, other than the sound of the swallows?'

Randall tipped her head to hear better and smiled. 'Grasses, whispering in the breeze and palm fronds clacking.' The smile slowly faded, her expression dismayed as she identified the qualities of each plant and tree and the lovers' knot design, formed by cotton lavender and golden marjoram. The plants might be more exotic, but its design and concept mimicked the garden they'd created at Broadfield.

Julio lifted her hand to his mouth and tenderly kissed her fingers. 'A sensory garden,' he said huskily. 'When I went home in the school holidays, I worked with the gardeners to make this garden, based on the one we'd created. I hoped...' He checked himself and started again. 'I hoped that every plant would be a delight to the senses. Perfume, exotic flowers and leaves, satin bark, rustling grass, peaches, nectarines, oranges. I designed this garden, for lovers—'

'How nice,' she said stiffly. Jealousy raged through her. Had he planned to bring Elvira here before it was decided he'd remain in Argentina? Was he thinking of living here with Isabel? They'd been *her* ideas! Not for him to enchant other women! Snatching her hand away, she started walking blindly along the path, calling back to him in a brittle tone; 'If you'll show me the rest of the areas you want me to design schemes for, I can then take some photographs and measurements.'

For the rest of the day she was on edge, waiting for something to happen. Nothing quite did—other than the occasional touch, an unguarded look, a tense silence. Yet those, the languid warmth and the enclosing embrace of the house, conspired to tear her nerves to shreds. When she returned and fled to the security of Ana's house and the comfort of Tom's innocent love, she felt a huge sense of relief.

And yet, even as she cuddled Tom, her mind turned to the house and the gardens, reliving moments she and Julio had shared, those occasional touchings, the unguarded, lingering looks and the warm murmur of his voice. He was becoming part of her life and she dreaded the day he returned to Isabel.

Every day that week, Julio drove her to the farm where they examined plans, argued, made decisions and tended the plants. With the help of a local man, they fenced in the goats more securely and, even in this simple task, Randall found to her concern that she was enjoying every moment she worked with Julio, their shared goal, their knowledge and love of plants a common bond.

The day before Tom's birthday, she took the usual roundabout route to Ana's. Making her way towards the sound of children's laughter, she mused that she valued her time with Julio as much as she treasured her time with Tom. The thought made her stand still in shock and clutch the newel post on the stairs. Closing her eyes she heard, in her imagination, Julio's rich, deep laugh, heard Tom's squeal... A chill froze her spine suddenly.

Those voices were outside.

With a cry, she ran into the shuttered kitchen and shakily eased back the louvre to see Julio in the garden with Tom. Her stricken eyes watched him as Julio played football with a bunch of giggling children, contorting his body in a comical effort to keep the ball bouncing on his chest.

'Oh, my God!' she moaned, cringing back and sinking to a chair. Her head whirled as though she would faint but she knew she daren't. When Ana ran in from the adjoining laundry-room, she turned angry, accusing eyes on her.

'No,' said Ana gently. 'I didn't ask him here. He just came, asked to see you, and said he'd wait when I told him you hadn't arrived.'

'I thought I'd always covered my tracks,' croaked Randall. She passed a hot hand over her even hotter forehead. 'What did you tell him?' she cried distractedly. 'Does he know I'm Tom's mother?' She groaned. If Julio was to find out, it must be from her, quietly and in calm, measured tones.

'He knows nothing. He's been playing with the children for fifteen minutes or so.' Her voice softened. 'I can see why you love him, Randall.'

Her head turned slowly towards the window. A wave

of desolation washed through her. He was showing Tom
how to flick the ball up with his toe and her son was
looking up at his father with trust and admiration on his
little face. When Tom failed in his first few attempts, Julio
appeared to praise and encourage him, his patient coach-
ing stilling Tom's trembling lip. There was a lurch of her
heart at Tom's eventual success...and then the ecstatic
child was in his father's arms, being thrown into the air
high—

'Enough to make the wind rush around your face,' she
said softly, tears blurring her eyes.

'What? Are you all right, Randall?' Ana asked, worried.

'I can't,' she sobbed. 'I can't tell him! I don't want to
lose Tom—'

Ana took her upstairs and gradually calmed Randall
then sent her to wash her face and called Tom inside. For
a while, Randall chatted brightly to her son—or rather he
chatted to her, talking non-stop while she tried to pluck
up the courage to face Julio.

'And he can do handstands all across the garden!' Tom
exclaimed, jumping up and down in excitement. 'On *one
hand*!' He paused, to give that the maximum of dramatic
effect and his small hot hand stole into hers. 'Come and
feel his muscles! He likes plants too. He knows a lot. I
asked him to come again and said he could be my daddy
if he liked.'

She fiercely bit back her cry, her teeth digging into her
lower lip. He'd bewitched her son too! There didn't seem
to be any justice in the world, she thought in despair. She
didn't want Tom to be hurt. 'What did he say to that?'
she asked huskily.

'He looked sad and said I had a daddy. He thinks Ana's
my mummy!' Tom laughed at the mistake. 'I was going
to tell him you and me were on our own and I'd def'n'tly
like him for a daddy if you didn't mind, but Ana called
me.'

It had come, thought Randall hopelessly. Tom would

be dragged into a tissue of lies if she didn't come clean. The doubts darkened her mind, frightening her, but she knew she had no option.

'Tom—' She forced herself to hold back the anguished screams that were gathering in her throat. 'Will you wait here, darling?' she asked in a strained voice. Tom's face fell and she knew with a pang of wretchedness that he didn't want to be deprived of his new daddy. 'Just for a few moments,' she said hoarsely. Luckily, Tom was too absorbed in thinking about his own needs to notice how strange she sounded. 'It won't be long before I call you and you can come down. It's something…special I have to do.'

'Special?'

Dry-mouthed, she drew her son into her arms, painfully aware that this would be the last time he was purely hers. Her hand brushed the raven hair from his forehead and she smiled shakily. 'I think all your dreams are going to come true, darling. So do wait.'

At the top of the stairs she paused, hearing the familiar roar of Julio's car. He was driving away. Stumbling down, she collapsed on the bottom step, all the wind taken out of her sails. 'I was ready to tell him,' she whispered to Ana.

'Can I come down yet,?' called Tom excitedly. 'Is my dream wish ready?' came her son's hopeful voice.

'Yes, darling.' Randall's mind went a blank. 'I told him I had something special to do, that all his dreams would come true!' she groaned, hearing the thudding of Tom's feet on the stairs.

'Here I am!' he yelled.

'The puppy,' prompted Ana.

'*Ohohohohohh*!' squealed Tom. 'For my birthday tomorrow?'

'You and your mamma will go out and buy one,' laughed Ana, as Tom hugged her and the shaken Randall together. 'Next time she has a day off.'

'You'll have a make-do present for tomorrow till we can choose your puppy,' Randall said huskily.

'And it can stay with the other puppies here, Tom, till you go to your cottage,' added Ana.

'Oh, you darling!' sighed Randall gratefully.

Overcome with emotion, she smiled through her tears and then went out to let the children tumble all over her. I can be happy without Julio, she told herself firmly, cuddling armfuls of hot, sticky children and pretending to eat a pair of fat dimpled knees.

But she was unable to convince herself. Tense and edgy, she put Tom to bed. She didn't know what to do now. She was spending her days with Julio, the rest of the time with Tom, and she loved them both. Grief flooded through her like a tidal wave. It was time, she thought bleakly, to start cutting him from her heart so that the pain would be less when he went—and his departure would have a welcome bonus. Tom would be back with her.

Shortly before midnight, she returned to Ronda. Seeing that the lights were still on downstairs in the villa, she swallowed back her nervousness and rang the bell. 'Sorry to disturb you,' she said politely, when a tousle-haired Julio opened the door. 'My friend said you were looking for me.'

He cradled a glass of whisky and by the look of him, it was nowhere near his first. 'Your friend said a lot.'

Randall chewed her lower lip nervously. 'What did you want?' she demanded, attacking when cornered as usual.

'Steve rang my agent. He wanted to talk to you,' answered Julio curtly.

'How did you know where I might be?'

'I've known where you went each evening for some time. I followed you once.'

Apprehensively she scanned his face for any sign that he knew Tom was her son but he seemed preoccupied with his own troubles. Her ploy of hiding Tom with other children had been successful. 'Sorry. I should have let you know.'

'I didn't expect you to keep to your word.'

She hung her head. 'Did Steve leave a message—say where I could contact him?' she asked anxiously.

'No,' Julio answered, and she had the feeling that maybe Steve had, but the information would never be passed on. 'Where were you?' he snapped.

'I was there. Upstairs,' she muttered resentfully.

'And seemed keen to keep that a secret. Were you with your lover?' he growled.

'No!' she said vehemently.

'Well something drags you there, night after night,' he muttered. 'And exhausts you so that you turn up every morning rubbing your eyes like a drowsy dormouse.'

'I—I don't sleep too well,' she floundered, thinking of her restless nights, aching for him.

'I gathered,' he snarled. 'You'd better go to bed. I'm expecting a lot from you tomorrow.'

She hung her head. 'I'll see you in the morning.' The weight of guilt sat uncomfortably on her. It would be his son's birthday. And he didn't know.

'Make it midday. I have a few things to do first. We'll have to pack everything in to the rest of the day,' he growled, eyeing his empty glass irritably. Randall wondered why he'd been drinking so much. Julio wasn't the kind of man to solve his problems in drink. He'd take *action*, fair or foul. 'Bring a change of clothes and whatever make-up you'll need for looking smart.'

'A prospective client?' she asked politely. He stared back at her in a strangely brittle way and didn't answer. Randall was too emotionally and physically exhausted to stay and ask questions. He'd tell her in the morning. 'I'll need to know if I'm going to be late,' she explained wearily. 'Ana will worry if I'm not there.'

A faintly sinister smile lifted the corners of his mouth. The hairs rose on the back of Randall's neck and her nerves did a quick shimmy through her body. 'Maybe. We can ring if we're delayed,' he said, his eyes glittering. 'Your lover will have to be patient.'

She flinched and gave him a sad, reproachful look. 'I—' She hesitated. His eyes pierced into her soul remorselessly till she was forced to lower her lashes to free herself of the urge to tell him what was on the tip of her tongue. This wasn't the time, not when he was belligerent from drinking. Already his face was contorting with rage at her delay in answering. 'I don't have a lover,' she said in a low tone.

His mouth thinned. 'You're not too good at lying,' he said contemptuously. He fixed her with a piercing stare that held her transfixed. 'Look, if this man really does mean everything to you as you once said, then marry him. I hate to see you behaving like a tramp. You're my partner and you represent the good name of my company. If he's already married, ditch him. If it's just sex, then I can provide that with more discretion—'

'No, Julio!' she said huskily.

He caught her wrist, dominating her with his eyes. 'It's only been the soft sell so far. How will you handle the next stage, I wonder?'

She licked her lips. 'I know how to cope with clients,' she rasped, deliberately misunderstanding him. She knew what he meant. His efforts so far had been mild compared to what he intended in future.

'We'll see,' he husked.

Hastily she said goodnight and backed away then ran down the path to the cottage. There was something in his promise that chilled her to the bone. He was planning trouble. Revenge: quick, hot, brutal. She shivered and went to bed with the feeling that a storm was about to break over her head.

CHAPTER NINE

RANDALL'S nerves seemed stretched thinly throughout the journey to the farm after they'd met at midday. It relieved her that Julio seemed disinclined to talk, though she was waiting on tenterhooks for him to make some reference to the previous night.

For several hours they planted saplings in the jewel-green fields to the glorious sounds of the wind whispering through the grass and the hoopoes calling from the stone pines, and it was a bittersweet time for Randall because they worked so well together, anticipating each other's needs, acting like a team. Or a couple who'd been together for years. She winced.

'Had enough?' asked Julio quietly.

'Can we call it a day?' she husked. 'I'm dying for a cold drink.'

'I'll top up the water in the buckets of unplanted saplings,' he said. 'You set up the drinks in the courtyard where it's shady.'

After a few moments, he joined her in the tranquil garden beneath a bower of bougainvillaea and honeysuckle. The drone of bees was all around them, and the wonderful fragrances that intensified towards evening. Rays from the sun were filtering through the palm fronds and tinting Julio's cheekbones and the appealingly crooked bridge of his nose. It was all she could do not to reach out and stroke his gilded face. She stifled a sigh, loving him so profoundly at that moment that it frightened her.

But Julio had known more powerful women, with qualities far greater than hers. His mother and Elvira had inspired love so deep that it had drawn two men across the Atlantic, away from this earthly Paradise.

'Penny,' murmured Julio.

She smiled gently. 'I was thinking,' she said, 'that your mother must have been a very special woman to entice your father from here.'

'She was,' he said, husky with the memory. 'Everyone loved her. No one even minded that she was the household maid. They all saw her qualities and—'

'*What* did you say?' interrupted the stunned Randall.

'The maid. Didn't I ever tell you?' he asked, amused at her astonishment. 'All her sisters are beautiful and pure. They married well, some to wealthy ranchers in Argentina—'

'The maid!' said Randall stupidly. 'Then—' She stemmed the words she had on the tip of her tongue. Why, she had been going to ask, didn't you marry me? 'So your father really did put love before everything,' she mused, a wistfulness in her voice.

Julio flinched. He sat staring gloomily ahead. 'I wish to God I had,' he grated softly through his clenched teeth and it was only Randall's ultra-sharp hearing that picked up the impotent fury of those bitter words.

She became very still, the breath shallow in her chest as she scanned his grim profile. 'Julio!' she said sharply. His head jerked around. 'You didn't marry for love?' she asked accusingly.

For an unendurable length of time his inscrutable gaze held hers and then she could see he was thinking, weighing up what he should do or say. He took a deep breath that swelled the whole of his ribcage and then on the exhalation came. '*No!*'

The word was expelled from his body as though it had been torn from his soul. Randall knew then, with a chilling horror, that his marriage had been nothing more than a union of two rich, proud families. A businesslike arrangement, which he'd gone into with his eyes open and regretted ever since, mocked cruelly by the happiness of his own father's marriage.

He was hard and ruthless. All through his life, she thought in dismay, he would weigh up situations, shutting out any sentimental regrets that might conflict with the Quadra dynasty. And to hell with the people he hurt in the process.

'What about Elvira? Did she love you?' she demanded tightly.

'No.'

Randall's hand flew to her mouth and her teeth grazed the knuckles. So cold, so hard, so *dutiful*. How could people be like that? He could have married *her*. She would have loved him till her dying day and... Her heart somersaulted. Dear God. He could have been a father to his son. 'You lied! You're always lying to me! It's a compulsion with you, isn't it? You told me that you'd married Elvira for both love and duty,' she said contemptuously.

'That's true. For love of my family. Duty to my family,' he said quietly.

'Oh, neat. A little twist of words here, a slight adjustment there and words can mean whatever you choose,' she said icily. How easy he'd fooled her! 'You ditched me to marry a dynasty, a *blood-line*! How dared you? I was flesh and blood and I loved you and you chose a pedigree instead of me! Did it tenderly dab your brow when you felt ill?' The rage turned her eyes almost black. 'Did it keep you warm in bed? Did it give you one half of the sexual satisfaction I might have done?' she rasped, losing control of her temper and discretion.

'*Dios*!' Julio's body was trembling with uncontainable anger. 'Don't judge me,' he snarled savagely.

'Oh, I'm judging you,' she said in contempt. 'Your perverted sense of duty to the Quadra came close to ruining my life. What if you'd had children?' she demanded. 'They would have grown up in a home without love, and that's unforgivable because you would probably have made them emotional cripples *like you*!' she spat.

There was a brief warning, as Julio's nostrils flared white and then he had caught her arms and was shaking her till her teeth rattled. 'Listen to me!' he seethed. 'I tried to love her. I needed love and comfort—God, how I needed it! If I could tell you why I married, I would. I swore on the sacred honour of the Quadra that—'

'Damn the sacred honour of your family! Take me home!' she raged. 'And forget the client you wanted to see. I'd bite his head off, the mood I'm in.'

'I can tell you this much. I had to marry her,' he rasped.

Had to…Randall swayed and Julio briefly steadied her then dropped his hands again at the flare of blistering anger in her eyes. A shotgun wedding was one scenario she'd considered and dismissed because of the time factor. In the tense silence, she struggled to voice her appalled thoughts. 'Was—' She swallowed back the nausea. 'Was Elvira—carrying your child?' she asked raggedly.

Julio stared, his astonishment genuine. 'No!' he growled. 'Come on, Randall, use your brain! That would mean I'd been making love to both of you at the same time—'

'I'd worked that out,' she spat. 'Had you?'

'No,' he said tightly, his eyes deeply pained. 'She was not pregnant with my child and I didn't two-time you. You were the only woman I ever looked at when we were at Broadfield. Look, this is hurting both of us,' he said huskily. 'Come and—'

'No!' She needed Tom, the comforting normality of Ana's house, not to be crucified with two of the most desolate words in the English language: *if only*. 'I want to go home. Don't speak to me. I might burst into flames!'

She strode grimly out to the car and collapsed on the passenger seat in abject misery. Julio followed, his manner grimly decisive. He thrust the key in the ignition. Nothing happened. He tried several times then got out and checked under the bonnet while Randall impatiently drummed her fingers on the dashboard, listening sullenly to the poignantly liquid song of a nightingale, drowning the croaking toads. She felt like howling.

'I think,' called Julio casually, 'we're in trouble.'

Randall glowered through the windscreen at him. They were in the middle of nowhere. It was Tom's birthday, she was tired and upset and his wretched car wouldn't start. Why did life always kick you when you were down?

'Let me try,' she said crossly.

He slammed the bonnet shut just as she came up to him. 'It's a job for an expert mechanic.'

'Well, at least let me try!' she snapped irritably, fiddling with the catch. 'I do understand engines, you know. I'm not a bimbo.'

'I know that engine inside out,' he retorted firmly, leaning heavily on the bonnet. 'It's a parts failure. Leave it. Come inside and wait while I call the garage.'

Randall stomped after him in exasperation. 'This is a nightmare!' she muttered. 'Ring for a taxi for me. I want to get home. On second thoughts, let me use the phone first. I must get in touch with Ana and tell her I'll be late.'

'Of course,' he soothed, a mocking smile on his lips. 'Dear Ana and the man upstairs.'

Randall irritably snatched the receiver and punched out the numbers, wishing she were jabbing his nose and crumpling it beyond its Brando beauty. 'Hello? Hello? *Oiga…*' After a moment, she lowered it. 'There's no ringing tone!' she said, mystified.

'*Really*? May I?' He listened. Then thoughtfully, his eyes lowered, he put the phone down. 'Well! How extraordinary!' he said in amazement. 'I'd better go and check the line. If it's down, I'm afraid you'll have to accept that we're here for the night.'

Apprehensively she waited, chewing her nails with anxiety. They couldn't be stuck. Not tonight—Tom was waiting for her, waiting to light his birthday cake. How far was the nearest house? Her agitation increased, her nerves strained to breaking point and she paced up and down, refusing to consider the alarming possibility that she'd be spending the hours of darkness here with Julio.

'Well?' she asked impatiently, when Julio returned.

'I'm afraid it's bad news. We'll have to stay here,' he replied, not sounding particularly sorry at all. She groaned. 'I'll go for help in the morning.'

'That's no good!' she said irritably. 'I can't possibly stay! What about discretion? What about the good name of our company?'

'I won't tell if you won't,' he said, hardly able to keep his face straight.

Randall's temper flared. It wasn't funny. 'Go now!' she yelled. 'Please!' she begged, when Julio didn't move. Tom would be frantic if she made no contact! 'You have to go!' she cried jerkily. It was his *birthday*. 'Don't you understand? I have to get to Ana's this evening.' She wrung her hands in panic, thinking self-pityingly of Tom's unlit birthday cake, his unopened present—and tormented herself still further picturing his mournful face, pressed to the window... 'I have to see To— Ana,' she corrected hastily. Julio was staring at her oddly so she tried to disarm him. Her smile was a little half-hearted, however. 'Please, try for me,' she wheedled.

'My, such loyalty to your nice friend,' he said sarcastically.

She fought for calm and failed. 'You must be able to get a taxi—a truck, a moped, a *bike*—I don't care. Anything!' she cried, her hands flying to grip his lapels and tugging urgently.

Julio's eyes narrowed. 'Such a fuss,' he drawled.

'It's a special date. A birthday...dinner,' she said, hardly knowing what she said in her distress. 'Julio, help me! He'll be disappointed if—'

'He?' queried Julio coldly. Cursing herself for the mistake, Randall found to her dismay that her wrists had been encircled by his strong hands. 'Who is this person you're so desperate to see?' he asked softly. 'Who is this Tom? When are you going to admit he's your lover, this man you sneak away for, stay overnight with, who means everything to you?'

Randall bit her lip as the increasing pressure on her wrists made her wince. 'I can't tell you,' she said stubbornly. 'Only that I have a good reason—'

'So had I,' he reminded her tightly. 'You couldn't put your faith in me when I claimed to have a good reason for marrying Elvira. Why the hell,' he growled savagely, suddenly exploding with anger, 'should I trust your word?'

'Don't do this to me, Julio,' she husked. 'You've hurt me enough—'

'You don't know what pain is,' he said softly. Randall's eyes widened in alarm. Julio gave a mirthless laugh, his eyes lethal. 'I knew if I put you under stress your guilty secret would emerge.' Julio's teeth clenched. 'Tom. When I called, you were upstairs making love!' he snarled.

'It isn't true,' she husked, frightened by the chilling revenge carved into every line of his face.

'Promiscuous women and deceit go together; I'd be mad to believe you. It seems that I don't have to step carefully over any barriers you've erected against me, or coax you to take them down. Now I know that you're a cheap little tramp, suddenly I find there aren't any barriers at all. Suits me fine.'

Randall struggled in earnest. He meant to take her, whether she agreed or not. His male pride would drive him to rape. She quailed at his daunting strength. Quick, hot, brutal...

'Let me go for help,' she grated, trying to keep her head.

'We don't need help,' he mocked. 'We can manage all by ourselves.'

Before she knew his intention, he had scooped her up

in his arms and was striding up the stairs while she kicked, struggled and yelled at him to put her down. Which he did, once he'd reached one of the bedrooms. His body barred the door and he turned the key in the lock with an air of terrifying menace.

'You can't possibly keep me here against my will,' she said defiantly, her face ashen.

'At this precise moment,' he snapped, 'I'm so angry with you that I'm capable of *anything*.' With a cry, she flew to the window and frantically jiggled the latch on the massive cedarwood shutter. Julio's hand closed over hers. 'You'd break your neck,' he growled. 'Is he worth it?'

She whirled to face him, knowing she was trapped and that the outcome of this night depended on how she handled the situation. 'Yes!' she wailed. 'I'd jump to escape being raped by you!'

'Rape?' He paled, visibly appalled, a nerve quivering by the corner of his mouth. 'Is that what you expect from me? That I mean to force you, like a thug in a back alley?' he asked hoarsely.

'What, then?' she husked, clinging to the last vestiges of hope. 'You'll let me go?'

'I can't. It's too late,' he growled. 'I intend to spend the whole night seducing you, achieving my objective, yes, and why not, when you give your body without shame? I remember how you made love,' he said, his voice honey-laden and throbbing. 'With a wholehearted, natural, uninhibited enjoyment and a willingness to explore the deepest pleasures we could give one another. I want that, for tonight. I want to swamp you in sensuality, torment you with your own passion until you yield and beg me to make love to you as though we were the only two people in the world.'

If only they were. Miserably, she took in Julio's haggard face and suddenly bleak eyes and felt an overwhelming sense of emptiness. Hot, scouring tears poured unheeded down her face, tears for her abandoned son and the awful end to the love she and Julio had shared.

'Don't cry,' Julio growled huskily. 'Oh, Randall, don't cry.' The rough tenderness in his voice only made her sob more loudly.

'Why are you so cruel to me?' she said raggedly. 'Why have you followed me, pursued me?'

'Because I want you,' he grated.

'And what you want, you get—or take,' Randall muttered. 'Because women like me are easy, aren't they?'

'Easy? You?' He lifted a sardonic eyebrow. 'You've held me off. Aroused me to such a pitch of desperation that I'll stoop at nothing to have you. This was to have been my last chance to make love to you. I'm going back to Argentina tomorrow. I couldn't go without...' His voice thickened with desire. 'Without taking you in my arms, touching your soft skin, breathing in the scent of your body—'

'Leaving?' she jerked in distress, betraying herself.

He froze in disbelief and then, 'Randall!' he breathed, his eyes glittering in triumph. 'Come here!'

'I can't, I won't—'

With a slow, animal grace, he walked towards her. She knew what would happen but was powerless to move. His brooding eyes seemed to ravish her where she stood, the desire spiralling inside her so fast that she was fighting for breath. And then she was in his arms, crying, sighing, safe, secure...

No. Not safe; how could she ever have felt that...?

In an explosive fury, he bent her backwards, possessing her mouth in a forceful, violent kiss that drove all thought, all reason from her head. She felt herself losing her balance. Emotionally, physically, mentally. The soft silk of the bedcover met her back, Julio drew her arms over her head and held them there, his eyes sultry black and frightening.

His mouth, tongue, teeth, limbs, all turned her skin into

a formless surface of sensation, her body arching into his wantonly and totally out of her control. Silent and urgent, he told her through his fevered kisses that he'd been driven beyond all means of return. She drowned in the remorseless attention, fought his hands as they skilfully removed her shirt and then his fingers touched her breasts and the hot, raging buds burst into bloom and Randall gave a deep groan of need.

'Tonight,' he muttered savagely, his eyes glittering at her. 'One night. I'll take just that. But my God, it will be such a night that you'll never know another like it!'

'Uhhhh—' Passion had stolen her voice. She found her mouth opening, lifting to Julio's with a will of its own.

A huge, shuddering breath trembled through his body and impatient, unstoppable, his mouth drove down on hers in an irresistible persuasion.

'I'll reduce you into such a mass of sensation,' he raged, a terrible hunger etching every line of his face, 'that you'll never forget this night for the rest of your life. Starting now.'

With the aid of his hands, his knee and the weight of his body, he imprisoned her limbs. Knowing that if she wriggled to escape she'd inflame him, Randall lay very still as he loomed menacingly over her and slowly ran an enquiring finger up the length of her leg.

She jerked spasmodically and he smiled, his dark head bending to kiss the sole of her foot, to draw each toe into his warm mouth, washing sensation over her with every breath he took. Languidly his lips wandered to the inside of her knee and his breathing became more laboured as he relentlessly savoured her satin-smooth skin, every second a little closer to triumph.

And then Randall felt the exquisite, heart-stopping caress touch her with an intimacy that defeated her totally. Her eyes closed and there was nothing, nothing in her world but the warmth of his mouth, the flame of this tongue and the violent contractions of her inner body.

'Julio!' she grated hoarsely, finding that her hands were free to clutch weakly at his hair. A gasp was wrung from her as a spasm shot through her from the unendurable slow torture. The rhythm of his touch increased, hotly inciting, till her greed could no longer be assuaged. She wanted more. She wanted him. 'Please,' she husked, with a little whimper, tugging at his hair, her head turning from side to side on the pillow. '*Please!*'

Gently he embraced her, his mouth soft, sweet on hers, the faintest of caresses keeping her body pliant for him. And with an impatient mutter, he caught hold of her skirt and slid it off in one quick movement, then the already torn delicate briefs that had been no barrier to his roving mouth.

'Love me,' he murmured huskily into her ear. 'Love me.'

'I do!' she moaned. 'There is no other man. There's been no one since you left! I've never stopped loving you, I do love you, with all my heart and I wish, I wish, I *wish* I didn't but—'

His body stilled. There was just the sound of his rasping breath and then she felt the shift of weight as he slowly rose from the bed. In the dim light of dusk, she watched Julio buttoning up his shirt and then sit tensely on the bed, his chest still heaving.

'You fool,' he said softly. 'Oh, you idiot—'

'What...?' She paused, confused.

There was a whirring sound. Dimly she heard it, her mind intent on their sweat-slicked bodies, the fact that she must have torn Julio's shirt open and eased it off, the fact that...

The telephone was ringing.

Randall's muscles tensed with shock. Her huge, bewildered eyes gazed accusingly into his. 'The phone!' she whispered.

Slowly he ran a finger over her stomach and let it drift

over the golden triangle of hair. 'Yes,' he said thickly. 'I forgot to disable this one.'

Randall's fingernails dug into his arms. 'It isn't out of order—'

'Correct. So sue me, sweetheart,' he husked.

Randall gave a ragged cry, lunged at the telephone, knocking it off the table and tried to pick it up, half in hysterics. 'It might be Tom!' she wailed.

'My God! You vicious bitch!' snarled Julio savagely. 'You *love* me? *You lying whore!*' He rolled away and sat on the edge of the bed, snatching up the phone and barking into it. '*Oiga!*'

Randall lay in silent shame while she listened coldly to a lengthy conversation. Then, numb and shaking, she sat up and found her clothes. The phone was working. Maybe there wasn't anything wrong with the car, either. No wonder he'd wanted her to bring a change of clothes and make-up. No wonder he'd brought enough food for the night and the morning. She'd been set up. She *hated* him, she wailed to herself.

Julio banged the receiver down, eyeing her with loathing. 'That was Ana,' he growled, still seething, his chest rising and falling rapidly.

'Ana!' she gasped. 'Yes. I gave her the number in case...' Her breath juddered in. It must be something to do with Tom. 'What did she say?' she asked urgently.

'Your damn Tom is ill. Food poisoning. He's in hospital.'

Randall gave a low moan and sank to the bed. 'Oh, Tom, my Tom,' she said brokenly.

His face set like stone, Julio contemplated her trembling, half-naked figure. 'He means that much to you?' he asked coldly.

She nodded, feeling numb with misery. 'Let me speak to Ana. Let me ring the hospital,' she sobbed.

Julio reached out and ripped the telephone from the socket. Then he dropped it to the floor in an extraordi-

narily helpless gesture. 'You're crazy about him, aren't
you?' he rasped.

Randall let out a low moan. If only he understood... 'I
would have been there with him if it hadn't been for you,'
she said plaintively. 'You bastard, you vile, evil bastard,
for luring me here, keeping me, when my—my Tom...!
Oh, I can't bear it!' Guilt-ridden, Randall fumbled helplessly with her crumpled clothes. Her hands were useless.
She lifted a forlorn face to the motionless, brooding Julio.
'How can I get to him?' she asked jerkily. 'There must
be a way!'

Julio scowled at her, his fists clenched. 'You really do
love him,' he said through white lips. Randall could only
sob and his hands slid beneath her armpits and he hauled
her upright, his breath rasping on her face in short, furious
bursts of heat. 'Tell me!' he roared. 'Tell me truthfully if
you really love him!'

'Of *course* I do!' she cried piteously.

For a moment, Julio appeared to rock on his heels and
then he was pushing her to the bed, dressing her with total
detachment as though he'd never felt any sexual desire
towards her at all.

With cold politeness, he helped her down the stairs and
settled her in the car. After fiddling under the bonnet, he
started the engine without any difficulty.

'You disabled the car deliberately—and the telephone!'
she whispered, appalled. 'What was it to be, your big
seduction scene? I'll never forgive you! Never!' she
raged.

Julio drove off like a man possessed. 'And I'll never
forgive you,' he said through his teeth. 'How dare you
pretend you love me?'

'Slow down!' she pleaded, terrified, as he took corners
at an unnerving speed. 'I want to get there alive.'

'For your darling Tom,' he muttered scathingly, but
eased up on the accelerator. He inhaled deeply. 'I loved
a woman with golden hair and a husky laugh that bubbled

out of her like a spring. She was everything to me. The breath of life—'

'Don't, please don't,' she moaned, almost broken with the poignancy of it all. He'd loved her and callously exchanged that love for duty.

'Shut up and let me drive,' he muttered. 'I'm close to murder in my heart and I'll have us off the road before you get to your darling Tom.'

She bit hard on her lower lip, keeping back the tears, but turning over and over in her mind the fact that he was driving her to the hospital where his son lay, ill, perhaps—

Randall drew in her breath with the sharp, agonising pain that cut through her heart. He had to know. He had the right. 'Oh, Julio,' she whispered in a guttural sound that came from her soul.

'What—?' Julio cursed, controlled the swerving car, and flicked a second concerned glance at her. 'What now?' he fumed.

'Something you must know. About Tom—'

'If I hear that bastard's name once more,' growled Julio ominously, 'I'll stop the car and you can damn well walk.'

'He's my son,' she whispered.

The car swerved out of control, then slowed. Julio stared straight ahead, intent on the road, crawling around the corners with the foggy concentration of a drunk. And then he pulled into a lay-by, stopped the engine and turned to face her. 'Your son,' he repeated coldly, his eyes quite dead.

'You said once,' she mumbled with difficulty, 'that we had...choices to make in life...sometimes between two things we badly wanted. I'm having to make one now...by choosing to tell you this.' She twice swallowed down the huge lump in her throat and tried to soften her dry lips. 'I—I want you to know that I'm telling you because it's my duty and not because I want to.'

'You're claiming that Tom is your son, not your lover.' Still his voice held no emotion. But she was aware that the evenness of tone was due to Julio's rigid control of his emotions. 'You realise that I'll come in and see this person with food poisoning and, if you're lying, I'll lay the two of you so flat that you'll need prising up with a crowbar?'

'Yes,' she said shakily. 'He is my son.' She watched Julio's eyes close, his jaw clench so hard she thought his teeth would shatter. And she braced herself for the next revelation. 'Don't you want to know who—who his f-f-father is?' she stuttered.

'*Dios*!' She could hear his breath rasping from his chest as if it were painful. A quick sideways glance at his face told her that he was seething with rage. 'Steve—'

'No!' she denied.

'So it's someone else. Why the hell would that interest me?' he said savagely. He started the engine.

Randall stayed his hand on the gear lever. 'I do want to get to the hospital quickly,' she said in distress. 'But…I haven't finished. You'll kill us both if you drive on now. Julio… Oh, God, don't glare at me like that!' she pleaded. He scowled into the mid-distance and she forced the words out fast before she could change her mind. 'Tom is *your* son.'

As if in slow motion, his head turned. She suffered his questing eyes bravely, every muscle taut with strain. 'No. I took care,' he said hoarsely. 'He can't be.'

'He is. I swear. Your name is on his birth certificate. It's his birthday today—'

'No,' he muttered. 'No.'

'I haven't known any other man,' she said in agitation, painfully aware of time passing. 'Steve knows. Ask him when he rings. He saw me right through my pregnancy.'

'*God*!' Julio's eyes glittered like hard black stones.

'Now can we go?' she wailed. 'Check with Steve later. He saw Tom when he was a day old, and nearly every day of his life after that—'

'What are you trying to do to me?' interrupted Julio,

his voice harsh in his throat with emotion. 'Another man, watching my son grow up… My son! Hell,' he muttered. 'Hold on!'

Suddenly, she was thrown hard into the back of her seat as he slammed his foot on the accelerator and the car lurched forwards, beginning a nightmare drive that had Randall sick with fear, her hands gripping the seat in terror while Julio aimed the car at the road like a bullet.

'Steve helped you?' he snapped in her direction.

'As a friend who took pity on me. He knew how upset I was because he was aware how much…how much I'd loved you,' she croaked. 'Get us there safely, Julio!' she wailed.

'I will,' he said grimly. 'God dammit! You kept my child's existence from me—'

'You were married! Should I have told your wife?' she cried.

'If you'd told me before—'

'Before what? You'd gone! All I had was a solicitor's letter!'

Julio cursed under his breath. 'How did you manage?' he grated.

'With the help of my friends. With Steve's support,' she said quietly. 'But I won't deny that it was a terrible time or that everything looked bleak and cold and heartless.'

There was a flare of Julio's scrolling nostrils as he inhaled sharply. 'You must really hate me to deny me my son.' Randall sat rigid with fear. Already he was sounding as if he meant to take total control. She began to shake. 'And now, because you leave him with strangers, he gets food poisining!' he seethed.

'Ana's not a stranger!' objected Randall. 'She's a dear friend. And what do you suggest I do? Give up my job and take Tom begging on the streets with me?'

'Don't be ridiculous. You should have applied to me for maintenance,' he snapped. 'You had my solicitor's address. It could have been done without Elvira knowing if that bothered you.'

'No. It wasn't only that,' she retorted. 'I didn't want my son growing up to be as selfish, arrogant, hurtful and callous as his father.'

'Oh, Randall,' he breathed harshly.

The car swept through hospital gates. With total disregard for any rules, he parked in a squeal of brakes outside the main entrance. Trembling all over, she stumbled out, was caught by Julio and frog-marched inside.

'*Estoy buscando a Tom...Slade,*' he barked at the receptionist.

While she obediently directed him, Randall tried to pull together the rags of her control, knowing she must remain calm and appear normal for Tom. Julio grimly steered her by the elbow along endless corridors while she tried to conquer her fears for her son's health. And his future. The hardest fight was to come. Her mouth quivered.

'Your son is sleeping,' said the doctor quietly to Randall outside his room. 'Please don't wake him, he needs the rest. But he's over the worst and he'll be fine in the morning. Children are very resilient.'

'I wish I were,' Randall muttered shakily.

Julio strode in ahead of her. Incensed that she was already being relegated to second place, Randall followed and was met by a relieved-looking Ana.

'It's all right, now,' she whispered. 'He was terribly sick and feverish but it's passed. We think he was treating a wounded hoopoe and was so excited telling us about it that he forgot to wash before lunch.'

Tenderly Randall gazed down on her son, hardly aware that Ana had tiptoed out. She bent to kiss his soft, rosy cheek. 'Poor darling,' she mumbled. 'On your birthday, too.'

A hand brushed Tom's forehead, gently, with the loving touch of a doting father. 'My son,' husked Julio, and Randall felt a rush of emotion as she looked from one to the other. Seeing his son had touched his heart. A terrible fear overwhelmed her. Julio's natural adoration of children would cause him to fight with all the means at his disposal for custody. 'My son.' He kissed Tom's perky nose and smiled. 'This is the little boy I threw into the air. I wondered why I felt such affection for him.' He sighed, his big hands close to Tom's on the coverlet. 'If I'd known, I would have helped you, Randall.'

'You would have taken my child!' she breathed.

Compassion filled his eyes. 'What you must have gone through, all alone at a time when...' As if unable to tear his eyes away, he looked at Tom and his face gentled with love.

'No,' she moaned. 'Don't look at him like that! He's mine! I won't give him up, not in a million years—'

'I want him,' growled Julio softly.

Her eyes closed in horror. 'Please, don't take him from me. I'm his mother—'

'I'm his father.'

'He knows me! I've brought him up! I paced the floor with him at night, worried over his health, taught him his numbers...' She heard her voice rising and took a couple of deep breaths. 'You can't take him away and let another woman care for him—'

'What other woman?' frowned Julio.

'Isabel!' she said piteously.

Across the sleeping form of their son, their eyes met and held. To her astonishment, he looked amused. 'I think she's a little young to care for a child,' he said gently. 'I should have told you who she is, I suppose, but your jealousy gave me hope. Isabel is a child herself.'

'A child...your child?' she asked, her mind whirling, trying to make sense of this.

'No. I'm going to break my vow to my family,' he said grimly. 'I think I've sacrificed enough. I won't have you thinking I'm a cold-hearted coward. I had to marry Elvira because she *was* pregnant—'

'I knew it!' she moaned.

'Hush!' he soothed. 'Someone else in the Quadra family was responsible, not me. Unfortunately, he was married.'

She blinked and stiffened, suddenly knowing who it was. 'Santini!'

Julio nodded, his eyes pained. 'My sister was playing prima donna and not spending any time at home. He was lonely, Elvira worshipped him...'

'I don't see why you had to marry her.'

'Honour, Randall,' he sighed. 'The disgrace of Elvira's family, the ostracising of ours if we didn't take responsibility for her. She was so very young. My heart went out to her. She was threatening to kill herself. She became ill, her unborn child was in danger. What could I do?'

Slowly Randall was beginning to see how hard it had been for him, how his concern for Elvira and her baby's life had driven him to take the honourable step. Her heart went out to him. 'Poor Elvira,' she said compassionately. 'It must have been so awful when she died.'

'Yes,' he said quietly. 'I felt very guilty that I hadn't been able to love her. After...little Isabel was very sickly for a long time and needed all my love and attention. I felt I owed it to her to be everything I could, to give her what I could.' His hand stretched out for hers. Tears of sympathy in her eyes, she reached towards it, their fingers entwining fiercely. 'I left it too late to trace you. With the school gone and you vanishing into the blue, I eventually gave up.'

And by then, he'd stopped loving her. Randall pushed back her hair from her hot forehead. 'I feel as if someone's run over me with a tank,' she said wearily. 'Julio, we'll need to talk about—about Tom,' she stumbled, trying to accept the difficulties that still lay ahead. 'Not now, please, I'm so terribly chewed up, but I promise I won't run away with him.'

'Randall—I never wanted to hurt you,' he said softly.

'But I thought you'd find it easier if you could hate me. That's why I never came to explain. And I knew I might abandon all thought of duty to Elvira if you cried even one tear and pleaded with those big blue eyes of yours.' He sighed. 'All this happened because of my cousin's stupidity. Because he hadn't considered the consequences.'

'Nor did you,' she said bitterly.

'Oh, but I did,' he answered, gazing into her eyes. 'My precautions weren't enough, but I was intending to marry you.'

'You want Tom,' she said in a small, broken voice.

'I want him. And I want you as well.'

'You said,' she muttered.

'You don't understand,' he said gently. 'When I saw you emerging from that lorry I was amazed, furious, bitter…jealous,' he admitted. He grinned crookedly at her. 'I was like one of my black bulls, charging around in a filthy temper. Then…I was angry with myself because I discovered that, despite the fact you seemed to be—ironically—ruining my sister's life by having an affair with her husband, I still loved you,' he said helplessly.

Randall straightened, suddenly alert. Her heart had skipped a beat or two. Now it was just skipping. She pressed one hand there, the other still enclosed in Julio's. 'Would you mind repeating that?' she asked faintly.

With great tenderness he smiled at her. 'I love you,' he said huskily. 'I tried to hate you, to despise you, to treat you like a slut, but all the time something inside me was saying that I was a fool, that what I felt for you was love and something far more than sex. When you said you loved someone with all your heart, I wanted to strangle you and him. That's when I knew I was in deep trouble,' he grinned. 'Serious love.'

'And you fixed it so that we'd be "trapped" on the farm,' she said slowly.

'Because one night with you would have been better

than nothing,' he husked. 'I was going to abandon all pride, pour out my heart and say that I love you, I always have, from the day I first saw you across the bonfire.'

'Oh, Julio!' she whispered.

'I began to plant the sensory garden at the farm when I was twelve, believing I would take you there on our wedding night and—' He chuckled. 'How's this for a young man's dream to end all dreams? I planned to kiss you, swig home-made lemonade and eat strawberries and ice-cream.'

Randall smiled in delight. 'Sounds wonderful!'

'Later, of course,' he murmured softly, 'I began to imagine more...intriguing things to do with you. Thoughts of you have tortured me for years. I wish I'd never hurt you,' he groaned.

'You gave me love, you gave me a son,' she answered simply. 'Your cousin must find it painful that his marriage is childless and his daughter is calling you "father". I know that in this country children are a way of life. I understand why he wanted to hear all about Tom at the interview. I feel pity for your cousin, Julio,' she said passionately.

'He planned to seduce you—'

'He gave me a job and brought us together again. You won't cut him up into little pieces, will you?' she begged.

'No. Only sack him and make sure he travels everywhere with his wife in future,' Julio said drily.

'Steve—' she began hesitantly.

'We'll get together when he returns and explain what happened. I owe a great debt to the man who cared for you and my son.' He smiled. 'I can hardly believe that I have a son to love and you to adore, Randall,' he said in a choking voice filled with emotion. 'I want you to be my wife. Let me telephone Isabel,' he urged, his dark eyes gleaming. 'I'll fly her over here so we can all be together.'

Randall's eyes became troubled. 'It isn't that easy to arrange people's lives. I don't know that it would be a good idea,' she said reluctantly, 'to tear her away from everything she knows. She'd be homesick. And—' She frowned, her stomach churning with nerves. 'Isabel might not like me and—'

'*Querida*,' he said affectionately. 'She'll adore you. I wouldn't have suggested the idea if I didn't think it would work. She's happy wherever I am—oh, and her pony,' he grinned. 'She's been pestering me for ages to visit Spain. I think I must talk about home rather a lot,' he added ruefully. 'My bloodstock director will be relieved to have me out of the way for most of the time so he can manage the ranch on his own. Oh, Randall, marry me, live with me at the farm that we both love so much.'

Dazed, she watched Julio kissing her fingers with gentle passion. 'I love you,' she said helplessly, seeing his eyes darken with desire. 'I'd live anywhere if you were there.' Her hand skimmed his cheek, the jaw dark and knee-weakening with his shadowy beard and her heart beat in a pounding rhythm as fast as the music of the *zapateado*. Softly their lips met.

'Is this my present? Is he my daddy?' came a sleepy voice.

Hastily separating, Randall and Julio laughed. 'Oh, yes, darling,' said Randall shakily, kissing her son on his cheeks. 'Happy birthday.'

'A daddy and a puppy too,' mumbled Tom, his lashes drooping. They fluttered up again. 'Can I have a sister next?'

'Happy birthday, Tom,' grinned Julio. 'And far be it from me to disappoint you—I think that can be arranged. A brother too, maybe?'

'Sleep now,' murmured Randall to her child, before Julio promised a football team. She began to hum Tom's favourite lullaby.

Two black, limpid eyes snapped open and fixed sternly on Julio. 'You won't leave Mummy, will you? The last one did.'

'Never,' answered Julio solemnly.

Randall felt a smile tug at her mouth and saw that Julio was shaking with laughter. Stifling their giggles, they fled outside then gave vent to their laughter till they clutched one another weakly.

He kissed her tenderly. 'I feel young again,' he husked. 'It seems years since I felt real happiness, real joy.'

'Like the old days,' she whispered, and he gathered her in his arms. 'Welcome to the ivory tower. I've waited for my prince to come for rather a long time.'

Julio gave her a dazzling smile. 'It'll be worth the wait, I promise,' he said lovingly. 'Tomorrow night, when Tom's asleep, we'll start on that bottle of home-made lemonade, the strawberries and ice-cream.' And then he began to tell her what he planned to do with them, till her blushes and breathless entreaties made him relent and he began to kiss her sweetly instead. 'I love you, Randall,' he murmured passionately. 'I love you more than my life. I'll take care of you and make you happy for as long as I live.'

With great tenderness, he led her to Tom's room again, where they waited contentedly dozing in each other's arms until the morning. And then, as a family for the first time, they drove to show their son the beautiful farm which was to be their home for the rest of their lives.

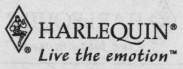

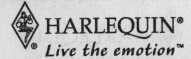

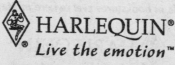

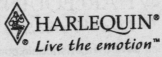

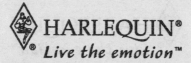

The world's bestselling romance series.

HARLEQUIN®

Presents

Seduction and Passion Guaranteed!

OUTBACK KNIGHTS
Marriage is their mission!

From bad boys—to powerful,
passionate protectors!

Three tycoons from the Outback
rescue their brides-to-be....

**Coming soon in Harlequin Presents:
Emma Darcy's exciting new trilogy**

Meet Ric, Mitch and Johnny—once three Outback bad
boys, now rich and powerful men. But these sexy city
tycoons must return to the Outback to face a new
challenge: claiming their women as their brides!

**MAY 2004: THE OUTBACK MARRIAGE RANSOM #2391
JULY 2004: THE OUTBACK WEDDING TAKEOVER #2403
NOVEMBER 2004: THE OUTBACK BRIDAL RESCUE #2427**

"Emma Darcy delivers a spicy love story...
a fiery conflict and a hot sensuality."
—*Romantic Times*

Available wherever Harlequin books are sold.

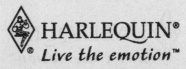

HARLEQUIN®
Live the emotion™

Visit us at www.eHarlequin.com